Women Who Overcame

2nd Edition of Struggles & Triumphs

History and fiction – After exhaustive research, the
author wrote these stories with creativity, leaving the
settings and women as accurate as possible.

H.M.

ISBN: 978-0-692-22276-8

To Ray -

My Husband & Friend

Women Who Overcame

Forward

We live in a broken world full of hardship and grief. The apostle Paul said all creation groans, as if in the grip of childbirth. Even those who know Christ groan. Maybe you lost a child or discovered you have breast cancer. Or perhaps you discovered an unfaithful spouse or your mother contracted a fatal disease. The blinding heartache might make you wonder if the battle is worth fighting.

I've been through tough trials too. My youngest child has severe disabilities, which hurts like swallowing razor blades for breakfast. My husband and I agreed we'd educate him at home with his siblings, and we did. What a difficult journey. During that time, I found history encouraging. The Lord used various stories from the past to give me the steam to keep going.

In the second book of Corinthians, Paul said, God gives us encouragement to pass along to others. I wrote my favorite historical stories to give my encouragement to you. During the publication of my first book, however, I walked through a series of horrific trials that lasted about four years. At times I wondered where God was, and I'd be jealous of my friends' happy moments. It started with my husband contracting encephalitis—an infection of the brain.

As you read these stories, you'll find a few unbelievers mixed amongst the Christians. I did that on purpose. The short-term victories pale as you compare them to those with eternal hope in the Savior. At the end, you'll find a snapshot of my story. I'm sharing it so you can see the hope I found.

For those who homeschool, I've grouped stories in the same era together in hopes that you can use the material as you teach history. Women stand in the shadows of history, and that makes research challenging. But I've given a good representation of the time period in which each lady lived.

So, friend, read and be encouraged. God walks with you through

Chapter One

Royal Crisis

Queen Katherine Parr, sixth wife of Henry VIII
1546
How can a wife obey a difficult husband? Katherine Parr did not want to be consort to the king of England. He divorced or executed his wives, yet a woman put her life in danger if she refused. Her position gave her opportunities to help the protestant cause. But what if she angered him and did not realize it until it was too late?

* * *

"Your Majesty, you must awake." A scraping sound assaulted my ears. The curtains? I stirred, but heaviness in my muscles screamed for more oblivion. Sleep sucked me back.

A hand shook my shoulder. "Ma'am. This is most pressing."

One glimpse showed the sun blazed through the multi-paned window beside the bed, searing my eyes. Its rays glittered over the gold candlesticks sitting by the bed and on the gilded frame of the king's portrait.

But I shrank back under the covers. The court kept late hours,

and I wished to sleep. After all, a queen should not have to endure an unwelcome touch.

"This document, your majesty. You must look, please."

Perhaps I experienced a nasty dream, unlike the luxury of a royal. Not that I was born in such a position.

"Please, Your Majesty!"

My maid? I opened one eye, and Mary Odell's face frowned with deep creases on her forehead. "What ... what?"

"My humblest apologies for waking you this early." Mary sank to her knees and bowed her head. "But this is most urgent."

"Urgent you say?" I stretched limp muscles and smoothed my black nightgown. Even if the king did not require my presence, I always wore the colors he preferred. "Stand up, my dear. I shall not hurt you. Henry might, but I have more respect for God's laws. Speak your concern."

"It's this, Ma'am" The maid held out a rolled parchment. "You must read it. I fear great peril."

Heaving a sigh, I shook my head. "You should. You've made great progress with your lessons. You read better than all my servants."

The maid's eyes grew large, and she stepped away from the bed. "Forgive me, ma'am. The ... lengthy words ..."

"Very well." Unfortunately, I tend toward impatience. It's something I always strive against. Being chosen as the king's wife made me less patient. I snatched the parchment and unrolled it.

My heart dissolved as I read my name as the king spelled it, Catherine Parr. No! I am innocent of any crime. Mary read enough to sense danger. "This is a warrant for my arrest."

Mary groaned and covered her mouth. "It's as I feared, Ma'am."

"Oh, God, what shall I do? My husband wants to throw me in the Tower of London." The same man courted me with professions of love. How many times did he compliment my slender figure and fair skin? I believed him, though I worried about my age. He even professed to like my auburn hair. Was it all a lie? God help me. I grabbed a wad of cover and yanked it closer. If only I could protect myself so easily. "Oh merciful Father, this is serious."

The maid bowed. "I await your command, Your Majesty."

"Where did you obtain this?"

The maid's face went white. After giving orders for three years, I could be too sharp. "Please tell me. I must know when and where as well."

"At the door, Your Majesty." She wrung her hands.

"At the door?" What an odd place to find a warrant. Could Mary be mistaken? Her face streaked tears and her hands shook. I must learn the entire story. "You mean the door to my chamber?"

"Yes. It lay on the floor in the hallway. I saw it when I entered, moments ago."

No one drops documents of import. This makes no sense. "Did you see anyone put it there?"

Mary shook her head. "No one was about, Ma'am. What can I fetch for you? A sip of water? Perhaps you'd prefer the comfort of your scarlet robe?"

"Send for my sister." I put my hand to my throat as the image of an axe appeared. "Tell her I am quite ill."

"Excuse me," Mary's chubby face wrinkled further. "You are ill?"

"Yes." I swallowed hard as I considered the fate of my husband's last wife. "Mortally ill."

I shall be in heaven, far from life's trials.

* * *

Someone tugged at my covers, and I peeked out. My sister stood at my four-poster bed. Her auburn hair and fair complexion mirrored my own. She ignored decorum, especially when driven to complete a task. I dealt with a crisis by removing myself. "Anne!"

"Sister, what ails you?" She pressed her lips together as she pulled back my blankets.

"Look at the scroll there beside me. I am doomed."

"What does it say?" She lifted her hefty skirt and sat on my bed. "Is this authentic?"

It took effort to nod, but I managed. If only I could find a place to hide. "I'd know the king's signature. I've seen him write it often enough."

Anne covered her mouth. "This is dreadful."

"I did not want to marry the king." I massaged my neck. What would execution feel like? "But one does not refuse His Majesty. Never anger the king, especially if he is your husband. He wanted me because I proved loyal, that is all."

"Yes. You proved yourself caring for your last husband. And despite your age, you are quite pretty."

"I reconciled myself to my position and tried to use it for good." I coughed against an annoying tickle. The image of the executioner wouldn't go away. "I brought the king's children back to court, taught them Scripture, and supported Protestant ministers."

"Indeed, I've seen you display the love of God to all you meet."

I shuddered. "Apparently my husband does not like something, and now I shall die."

"No." Anne rose and paced. "We must devise a plan."

I sank down and pulled the covers to my neck. "My funeral? I know my fate."

"Sister, this won't help."

Tears leaked onto my pillow. "If only I married Thomas, but he could no longer court me once the king singled me out."

"Forget Thomas Seymour." Anne's face grew red. "You are married to the king. Did you anger him?"

"We often discuss the Bible and the Church of England." A muscle

"My illness, if you wish to call it that, resulted from bad news." I gave her a summary of the situation.

The duchess gasped. "Oh no!"

I threw myself into her arms and allowed the tears to flow. She rubbed my back until my weeping subsided into sniffles.

"There, there, dear friend." The duchess pulled away and placed her forefinger on her face. "Let us seek the Lord. May I?"

"Please."

The duchess bowed her head. "Almighty Father, I praise you for your sovereign rule over the universe. What a joy to have access to the throne through your Son, Jesus Christ. Our anxieties never alarm or dismay you. Give us dispassionate coolness while we consider our options."

"Thank you." If only I didn't shrink from unpleasant situations, but I acquired the habit with practice.

"Now, we must consider." She bit her lip. "Doctor Wendy said the king might relent should you apologize."

"Yes." I nodded. Had I ever seen the duchess intimidated? Her courage made my pulse speed up. "But I believe with all my soul in redemption through Christ's blood. I prefer to die rather than deny that."

"No. You mustn't do that." She scrunched up her face. "Did the king discover any forbidden books in your rooms?"

"I had them all removed, besides, he never gave anyone permission to enter my quarters. Doctor Wendy reported His Majesty upset because I advised him to institute further reforms to the English church."

"Go on. Tell me more."

"His Majesty told the good doctor that I saw myself as an expert and dared to advise my husband."

A smile radiated across her face. "Ah, there is something we

can use!"

"What?" I saw nothing helpful, but facing one's death interfered with reasoning.

"A king or a husband would resist the idea of someone dictating instructions. You can apologize for that—without denying the gospel."

"Indeed!" I clasped my head in my hands. "What an excellent solution. If only I realized the impact of my demands, I would not be in such a tangle."

"My dear, I know you well." She ducked her head. "I daresay you wanted the king to understand the need to trust in Christ for his own salvation. You've spoken of that often enough."

"That is true. I exercised caution at first, but His Majesty never reacted. So he saw the extent of my zeal."

The duchess nodded. "God's word states women should be submissive to their husbands, and we want to obey. Instructing them doubtless oversteps the bounds. I've done it as well, but my husband does not wear the crown."

Anne sprang to her feet. "I shall accompany you, sister. Should we dress and speak with the king anon?"

The duchess glanced over to the window and motioned to the fading light. "It is growing late. I suggest you approach him tomorrow. After sleeping tonight, you'll feel much better.

"Aye, after much prayer and sleep."

* * *

My heart banged about in my chest before the sun rose. My actions today would seal my fate. Would the king transport me to the Tower of London for trial, or would he forgive me? I massaged my neck. It wasn't very large. Could an executioner take off my head with a single blow? Nausea rose.

I descended from my bed and dropped to my knees, quaking all over. "Almighty Father, guide me today. Give me favor in the eyes of the king."

Mary Odell appeared at my side as I rose. "What can I do for you, Ma'am?"

"Prepare a milk bath and bring my sweet-smelling herbs." I unfastened my braid. "Today I shall go to dinner, but I must dress exceptionally well."

She nodded. "And which gown?"

"I want the red brocade with the square neck. The bell-shaped sleeves are lined with ermine."

"A good choice."

I brushed my hair till it shone and soaked in my bath for some time. Afterward, my maids anointed my entire body with sweet smelling herbs.

Shortly before mealtime, I glided to the king's chamber accompanied by my sister. The pulse in my throat pounded as fast as a woodpecker attacking a tree, and my breath came fast.

The king sat in his huge chair, his bandaged foot elevated on a velvet cushion.

"Good morning, Your Majesty." I bowed. *Oh, Father, come to my aide. I would rather dash away, but I must face this.*

"Katherine." He smiled. "Do you feel better this morn?"

I lowered my head. "I feel much better, but my own folly brought it on. You see I fear I angered you, and I wish to apologize."

His eyebrows rose, and his chest swelled. "You no longer demand I do what you wish? Perhaps you should wave a Bible under my nose. I might need correcting on some point."

I shook my head. "That will not be necessary. You can read it for yourself."

He leaned forward and pointed to me. "Should I have you ordained as the First Lady Minister?"

"No, Sire. I do not have superior knowledge, but I shall discuss

whatever you please if it distracts from your discomforts, my husband." I clasped my hands at my waist, hoping the king did not see the tremor. "But I have nothing I must teach you."

The king extended his arms. "Then dear wife, I forgive you. Come, massage my shoulders. Those knaves of mine cannot do it correctly."

A pang of joy radiated through my chest as I hurried to him.

"Give me that black velvet box, boy." The king pointed to the chest across the room.

The servant bowed and placed it in his hand.

"Katherine, I know you like red." He opened the box and a ruby ring glittered in the sunlight. "I had it made for me, but I shall have my man fit it to you."

"Thank you, Sire." I kissed his cheek. "That's exquisite."

His bulky body turned to face me. "What a bonny smile, Katherine."

The door flew open. "The Lord Chancellor and his guards, Your Majesty." Lord Wriothesly and Lord Chancellor marched in with six armed military from the tower. They carried swords and spears. "Your Majesty, I am here to make the arrest, as you ordered." The chancellor held a document aloft.

The king waved his arm. "Leave me and take your men."

The chancellor blinked several times.

"Enough! Go now."

The man turned and fled with his soldiers.

I patted the king's shoulder. "Those poor men seemed scared."

"They came for you, my dear." Henry took my hand. "But they cannot have you. You are my excellent wife, and I shall escort you to dinner."

Epilogue

Spelling wasn't standardized in Tudor times. While reading documents from that era, one word will be spelled several different ways. For instance, sinner could be spelled synner, siner, or Sinner. The queen spelled her name Kateryn, although others at the time spelled it Catherine or Katherine. Katherine's tomb at Sudeley Castle reads: Here Lyeth Quene Kateryn wife to Henry the VIII …

Katherine came to court often since her mother served Henry VIII's first wife. When Katherine found herself an object of the king's attention, she was a widow. At the time, she was in her thirties and in love with Thomas Seymour. Katherine married him after the king's death in 1547.

Chapter Two

Mortal Danger

Catherine, Duchess of Suffolk
1556

Queen Mary, the oldest child of Henry VIII, ascended the throne in 1553. An outspoken Catholic, she imprisoned Protestant ministers and threatened anyone outside the Catholic faith. Catherine, Duchess of Suffolk, and her husband, Richard Bertie, treaded with care to avoid a fiery death.

* * *

Candlelight cast eerie shadows over Richard Bertie's face as he strode into the darkened library. Catherine, Duchess of Suffolk, bit her lip as her husband approached. English politics created complications these days, and something about his expression set her on edge. "Is there a problem?"

He gave her a curt nod. "We have a summons."

Catherine groaned and dropped her quill, splattering ink on the paper before her. "How alarming."

Holding up a parchment, he crossed the thick woolen rug. "This just came from Stephen Gardiner. He called us to meet with him."

Catherine lived amongst the upper class all her life. Her mother served Henry VIII's first queen, and her father was a courtier. Until now, she avoided unpleasant clashes. She ignored the slight tremor in her hands as she pushed her chair away from the engraved walnut desk. "What does it say?"

Bertie pulled up an ornate chair beside her. "It bears the seal of the Crown, and it demands we present ourselves at the palace before the Lord Chancellor, Stephen Gardiner."

"May I see?" She leaned toward light from the candelabra and scanned the writing. "Exceedingly wicked. That man is evil."

Bertie cleared his throat. "I have been expecting this."

Wrinkling her nose, she tossed the paper toward her husband. Richard Bertie, a graduate of Oxford, gained her confidence when he managed affairs for her first husband, the Duke of Suffolk. After the Duke passed away, she sought Bertie's guidance with her husband's estate. "We must consider our daughter. Do you have any thoughts on our response?"

Her husband narrowed his eyes, a typical expression when deep in thought. "This political shift came so rapidly. In the past, your husband's reputation during Henry's reign gave us a good name. This document could mean our lives are in danger. We must consider our options."

"Aye!" Catherine nodded as she placed her forefinger on her cheek. One must make careful choices in such a dangerous time. "They imprisoned Reverend Latimer over a fortnight ago."

Bertie rescued the document from the floor. "He knew the risks, Catherine."

"I do worry for him. Over and above his kindness to us, I feel in debt to him since his sermons brought me to saving faith. He sought to free all England from the oppression of Popery." She traced the gold braid on her sleeve. What a useless frivolity at such a moment. One wanted to live rather than die at the stake. "I've had servants deliver meals to him in prison."

"A good choice, my dear. But if I'm correct, the new queen will take issue with your actions." Bertie wore a frown as he took his wife's hand in both of his. "We aligned ourselves with the Protestant cause. I believe Queen Mary is determined to make England Catholic again."

Why was it suddenly so cold? "Doubtless, she wants revenge for what her mother suffered at the hands of her father."

"I've watched the trends, and I agree. Revenge is a tricky thing and could produce a backlash, which could damage the queen politically." Bertie rubbed the back of his neck. "At this point she's resorted to torture to alter her subjects' opinions. What a poor choice."

"Aye." Catherine raised an eyebrow. "She certainly will not change mine."

Bertie groaned. "I know, my dear. But your distaste for Stephen Gardiner could have been a bit less obvious."

She leaned away, pushing aside the clammy void in her chest. "What do you mean?"

He licked his lips. "The dog. I am sure you could have contrived another name for our dog."

"I think the name Gardiner is suitable for a dog. The man himself fails to act human most of the time." She sniffed. "My dog behaves with more manners than he even knows."

He spread his hands. "I agree, but perhaps a less personal attack on him would have been better. Now that he regained power, we may be in mortal danger."

"Darling, if this is about our faith, we would still be in danger even if I named the dog John. I've used my influence and considerable estate to promote the Gospel." She rubbed her hands together to bring back the warmth. Giving in to oppression never worked, and she would fight as long as she could. "Our faith is the core of our lives, and we must not waver."

"I agree, dearest. I shall never renounce my faith in Christ. Besides, I prefer to raise my daughter with the tenets of Scripture."

"Indeed. Just think—I could never have married you as a Catholic. Church leaders would have prevented it since you are beneath my station." Catherine released a sigh as unpleasant images appeared in her mind. "Can you imagine how much joy we'd have missed?"

"We do have the advantage right now. The country holds us in high esteem and the Crown must convince them we are traitors. However, if we are convicted of treason, the Crown could seize our estate. Queen Mary would be pleased." He punched his right fist into his left hand.

"I cannot help but think of Queen Katherine." Her chest was heavy. If only she still had her dear friend. "How much Mary loved her. I wonder if the Queen, had she lived, would be able to soften Mary now?"

He grimaced and shook his head. "Nay, Mary is adamant. Her mother received evil from Henry, and she wants to restore her mother's church."

Catherine threw up her hands. "Then what? We must also remember our daughter. Whatever we do, we must find a way to protect Susan from danger."

He paced the length of the room. "If we appear, we must have a reason to visit the continent. As yet I do not know what that is."

She extended trembling hands to him. "Dearest, come! We must pray for guidance."

In the semi darkness, Catherine adjusted her skirt and knelt by the desk.

Her husband knelt beside her. "Father, our lives are in danger. "Please give us wisdom," Bertie prayed.

* * *

Catherine's body jerked as the red-uniformed soldier opened the door. She blotted her sweaty hands with her handkerchief. If only this ordeal were over. Why did she name her dog Gardiner? At the time it seemed a nice joke. No one dreamed Gardiner would come to power again and place them in danger. In the past, she spoke her mind and never worried about what anyone thought, but that was when Henry was king. She never thought she'd wish for his reign after his death.

She and her Bertie traveled from their country estate in Lincolnshire to Barbican Manor, their home outside London. They had been waiting in St. James Palace to see Stephen Gardiner.

"The Lord Chancellor will see you now."

She glanced at Bertie. His jaw tightened, but otherwise his face wore a mask of calmness. Together they rose and entered Gardiner's office. Her skin prickled.

Gardiner sat behind a massive desk inlaid with oak and walnut. Two carved wainscot chairs sat in front of it. Sun streamed through huge bay window across from his desk making the room almost too warm. A uniformed page hovered at Gardiner's elbow with a stack of papers. An ordained priest, the Lord Chancellor wore a clerical robe—a full white gown gathered into a yoke below the neck worn over a dark undershirt. His long beard and thinning hair made his oblong face look almost square. His drooping eyelids made him look very sleepy. "You came at last. I expected you yesterday."

Bertie bowed. "Your summons arrived at dusk. The trip from Lincolnshire is about eighty miles. We made haste and arrived late last night."

The Lord Chancellor opened his lids wide revealing his dark eyes.

debt?"

Her husband shrugged. "Aye. And we have tried every method possible to retrieve the money. I must do it in person."

The sagging skin around Gardiner's mouth curled into a smile. "I shall have my secretary prepare a pass for you. The duchess must stay here, of course."

Catherine held her breath. Would he let them both go home?

"Thank you, sir!" Bertie bowed and turned to leave.

"One moment." Gardiner stood and his wrinkles appeared to harden. "I must know how to contact you."

"We are staying at Barbican Manor, just outside London." He clutched his wife's arm and they left the room.

Once inside their carriage, Catherine released a huge sigh. "Our plan worked."

"Quiet, dearest. We have no idea who might overhear." He took her hand. "Once I am in Europe, I can find a safe place for us. Then I shall send word for you to come. You should be safe at Barbican Manor while I'm gone."

* * *

Catherine's hands fingered the long string of pearls hanging down the front of her red silk gown. She stared out the sitting room window, searching the horizon. If only she could receive a letter or note from Bertie. He left six months ago, and she'd heard nothing. Was he safe? Or did he encounter some accident? Images of him filled her mind. Her clever husband would devise some way to contact her. Surely she would have heard if danger befell him.

Snowflakes drifted down from the sky like cotton and rested on the bare limbs of the trees. Robins walked across the snow of the landscape. A well-bundled servant tramped past, but Catherine saw no one else.

Once again, oh, Father, I pray for Bertie's safe return.

The housekeeper entered, lip curled. "Duchess, a tradesman insists on speaking to you. I tried to send him away, but he would not go. Shall I call the sheriff?"

The duchess held her breath and turned. She must keep her poise so no one suspected her fears. Was all the tension worth it? Should she just give up and let herself be thrown in jail for her faith? "Did he give you a name?"

The housekeeper wrinkled her brow. "I paid little attention, but it started with a 'c.' Was it Craddock? No, Conwell."

"Aye, that is the man." Her heart did a somersault, but she willed her face to display a placid reaction. "The Duchess of Sussex promised to send a salesman who could obtain rare type of silk. Send him up."

The housekeeper nodded and returned with an elderly man with short gray hair, a rounded face and a long crooked nose. "Madam, this is George Conwell."

Once the door closed, the elderly man stepped forward, "Greetings—"

"One moment." She tiptoed to the door and glanced up and down the hall. "Aye, we are alone now. Do you have news from Bertie?"

He pulled a sealed paper from his jacket and placed it in her hand. "I do. He gave me instructions. It must be burned after reading."

She broke the seal with trembling fingers, unfolded the paper and read it several times. "Dearest Bertie, it is so good to see your handwriting again."

At last she tucked the paper in her skirt and looked up. "I'm sure you know he's summoned me. When do you think I should leave?"

He waved his thin hand. "We must be gone tonight."

She sucked in her breath. "But why the speed? I must make plans, gather clothes. And there is little Susan to consider."

He leaned closer to her and handed her a map. "I believe your life is in danger. Choose two or three servants you trust. You should plan to leave just after dark and meet me at Broken Wharf. I shall have a small boat to take you down the Thames."

The duchess crammed the map into her pocket and sank onto the couch. Possibilities popped into her mind. She must know the problem. "What do you suspect?"

He raised his scraggy white eyebrows. "You have a spy, maybe even two, amongst the servants."

She touched a finger to her cheek as she mulled over his words. "I thought so."

"I would not trust anyone who tends to be too curious about your activities, or that you have not known for years."

She closed her eyes and nodded, almost feeling the flames leaping up her legs. No! What would happen to her daughter? Besides, she had no guilt that deserved such a death. "That describes my housekeeper. She watches me closely."

He extended his hand to her. "Your husband entrusted your safety to me. Be very careful."

She pulled the letter from her pocket and kissed it before she tossed it in the fireplace.

Lord, protect us.

* * *

Trying not to make a sound, Catherine hovered in the evergreen trees midway between the house and the road. Since the sun set early in winter, she left the house just after dark. Conwell arranged their departure so they would catch the tide going out the Thames, and she gave herself plenty of time to find him. While slipping through the yard, a twig cracked. Her gaze peered into the blackness. If only she could see.

The maid, Maria, who held her toddler, whispered, "Madam—"

"Sh-sh-sh! If we are caught now, they will arrest us."

A whimper. "Dearest Susan, you must be silent," the duchess

26

whispered as she patted the bundled child.

Moments seemed like hours and her heart pounded with such intensity she feared it would betray their position. Would death be better? She closed her eyes and imagined.

No. She would not allow anyone else to raise Susan. They must escape. *Precious Savior, help us!*

After waiting and straining to hear, she squared her shoulders and leaned toward Maria's ear. "Follow me. Quietly!"

The two ladies crept across the yard to the gate that a faithful servant left unlocked. The hinges creaked.

"Who goes there?"

"Quick!" Catherine grabbed Maria's arm and pulled her into the road just as light flooded the yard.

"Hello?"

Catherine rushed Maria into thick evergreen shrubbery across the road. Footsteps crunched in the frozen grass they'd vacated.

"Mama!"

"Sh-sh!" Catherine's mouth was like cotton and her skin icy despite her heavy cloak. She could feel Maria's breath on her neck and smell the pine scent of the shrub.

"Madam, I dropped the bundle of Susan's clothes—inside the gate," Maria whispered. "Should I fetch them?"

"No!" Catherine's stomach lurched. They would have to purchase clothing in Europe. "It's too dangerous. Stay here until they walk back to the house with the lantern."

The moments ticked away—each one lasted twice as long as they should. The wind moaned through the trees, and Catherine gritted her teeth to keep them from chattering. At last the light faded and the footsteps died away.

She put a trembling hand on Maria's arm. "Now come with me."

Catherine and Maria tiptoed out of the shrubbery and down the

his belt. The bag held a small loaf of bread. "Here, this should work for now. We will go ashore and then be on our way soon, Mrs. Fitch."

* * *

The acrid taste of vomit lingered in Catherine's mouth, and her stomach churned. Their ship ran into a storm, and the wild pitching on the waves had been too much. She rested, eyes closed, in the captain's cabin on a thin mattress stuffed with straw. The wind and waves lashed the ship, rocking it back and forth. She was thankful the captain had his bed secured to the floor. Bertie had arrived in Leigh on the Sea, and their trip across the channel began just after dark. "Dearest?"

She tried to rise onto her elbow, but nausea gripped her again. At least Susan slept unhindered by their adventure, the waves her rocker.

Her husband staggered with the lurching of the boat as he made his way to her bed. The boat creaked and moaned. "The captain is worried, dearest."

She swallowed hard before she answered. "What's wrong?"

"The wind is blowing us back toward England."

The duchess covered her face. After overcoming obstacles to get here, their efforts might come to nothing. Where was her loving God? She banished such thoughts from her mind. "God help us."

Her husband now stood over her bed hanging onto the rafters to keep his balance. A deep frown creased his brow. "Dearest, I devised a plan to outsmart Gardiner. And Conwell concocted a way to avoid officials in Leigh. I managed to arrive at Leigh undetected, and we both used our wits to get aboard a ship leaving England. But I cannot devise a plan for this storm."

She frowned, took his hand and squeezed hard. "Going back to England now will be fatal."

"Yes. The Queen will execute us both." He grimaced, and the veins stood out in his throat. "We must pray, dearest. God alone can help us now." He sat on the bed and took her hands in his.

Bertie prayed first. "Almighty Father, we sought your face and you guided us. We have no control over the storm and so we can do nothing more. Death does not hold terror for us. We would be in your presence because of our faith in Christ. But we ask for you to protect us from the injustice of Queen Mary."

"Precious Father," Catherine prayed, "we acknowledge that we are made of dust. You have the power to take life or save it. I am unable to stop a storm, only you can do that. Convey us safely to Europe. And give us comfort in this storm," Catherine prayed. "Help us to further the cause of your kingdom. We rely on your wisdom and protection, regardless."

She opened her eyes and wiped tears from her face. Her husband did the same.

"I brought a copy of the Scriptures. Let me read to you."

She lay back again on the bed, and he sat down beside her, and read.

Two hours later Conwell stepped inside.

Bertie called. "Hello. Any news?"

Conwell smiled and his blue eyes danced. "The captain said the storm is subsiding and the wind is shifting. We can now see continent, and we will land in less than an hour.

A radiant smile broke over Bertie's face and he kissed his wife.

"Praise the Lord!" Catherine applauded.

"Amen!"

Epilogue

Catherine and Bertie stayed in Europe until Queen Mary died, and returned when Elizabeth ascended the throne. Despite her association with Protestants, Elizabeth I didn't make all the reforms Catherine hoped for. The duchess believed the elaborate ceremonies

the bright sun.

Katie eased to her feet. It took more effort. Yes, she must teach one of her girls this job. "I'm here."

"Hello." His long face broke into a grin. "There you are. A beggar lady came asking for food. She's at the front door, but she appears to be ill. What should I do with her?"

Katie brushed off her hands as she inhaled the mingled smells of tomato plants and fresh soil. Even though it was September, she'd heard rumors of the plague in Wittenberg. If she brought this woman in, everyone in the boarding house would be at risk. Besides, with the baby coming soon, she preferred caution. Images came to mind of her daughter, Elizabeth, who died during the heat of August three years ago. "Fritz, I do not see how I can add one more person to my house."

"But what can I do for her?" His smile melted into a frown.

God commanded his people to love those less fortunate. How could she do that and protect her family? Fritz will want specifics. "Offer her some cheese and bread. Then send her on her way."

"I am sure Doctor Luther would approve." Fritz bowed his lanky frame and hurried back to the house.

She squatted slowly and turned to the pumpkins and squash. The roses came last, if she had time. The cool weather had not decreased their blooms yet, and flowers from her garden lightened the former monastery.

Her gaze landed on the herbs nearby, and the destitute beggar popped into her mind. In the convent, she studied herbal preparations and now she had a knack for concocting medicines of all sorts. She often treated her husband for various ailments. Did she make the right decision about the vagrant? Surely inviting disease into a full house would be unwise. But Jesus loved her when she was a sinner and not winsome.

Contagion

"Katie? Katie?" Her husband's voice rang out over the garden.

She looked up. Luther stood beside the thick wooden door that Fritz had entered a few minutes before. He carried an armful of books and wore a dark robe that went to his knees. She lumbered to her feet once more and waved. "Here, Doctor."

He came toward her. "I found an indigent at the door, and I installed her in the room on the second floor by the stairwell."

"But that is the room I prepared for the new student who is coming in tonight." Her husband lacked the tenacity to hang onto things. She'd hidden her silver platter so he couldn't gift it to his friends. Now he'd given away a bedroom she'd prepared for the new boarder. "Isn't she sick? Fritz was just here talking about a beggar. I do not want to infect the entire household."

Her husband grimaced as he shifted the pile of books in his arms. "We cannot turn her out. Jesus died for her."

Katie's face grew hot. "But what will I do?"

"You will take care of her, of course. I know how clever and resourceful you are. Look at you. Not many women would garden in your condition. You will think of something. But I have a lecture." He bustled off.

Katie opened her mouth, but no words came out. Staring at the back of his dark robes, she watched him retreat into the house. When they married, he announced he didn't marry for romance, but after several years of marriage she thought he loved her. If only she could ignore that inner desire to be cherished and adored. Her excellent nursing secured his respect, but he commanded her to use that skill, in spite of the danger. Sometimes she almost wished she'd married one of the other professors. Right away she shoved that thought away. What an honor to be Luther's wife. She must thank God daily for a godly husband and overlook his faults.

She tried to think of a plan. Already seventeen people lived in their house, and another student would come today. She had four teenage nieces and nephews from her sister's family, her aunt who had also escaped the convent, a widowed mother along with her offspring, her own children, and university students who paid rent.

Soon she must see to dinner preparations, but her husband commanded her to nurse an intruder who might very well have the plague.

An obedient wife would do this job right away. On the other hand, Hilda would be perfect. Even though a new employee, she was quite clever and proved her worth at housekeeping. This could be a great opportunity to see how well she catches on to doctoring. There's always a need for that. Doctor Luther was pleased that she'd found a way to hire another orphan, and he'd commend Katie for adding to Hilda's knowledge.

Katie straightened and rubbed her sore muscles as she admired her completed work. No one could do this as well. However, delegating various other duties demonstrated wisdom and kept the household running.

Aunt Lena appeared with both children. Strands of her gray hair escaped her bun and dangled about her wrinkled cheeks.

"Katie, the children have been good, but I need a rest." Her elderly aunt had worked in a convent for years and expected immediate obedience.

"Thank you! Now get some rest, Auntie. You look tired." She watched her aunt hobble back to the house.

"Mommy, I hungry!" Her son, Hans, scurried toward her.

Magdalene toddled a few steps behind sucking on her fingers.

"Hans!" Katie kissed him, rumpled his dark brown hair, and then reached for his sister.

"Hongry mommy! Hongry!" Magdelene said.

"We will eat." She held her daughter's small body close to hers.

Contagion

Magdelene's soft blonde hair smelled like the outdoors. They had been awake since six. She should feed them before serving dinner and put them down for a nap.

Her son raced toward the house shouting.

"Hans, come back. Let's wash our hands at the fountain before we eat." Luther's friend had found an ingenious way to pipe the spring into various parts of the city. A fountain in their courtyard provided water for washing and cooking. She led both children over to the fountain. Her kids splashed water all over themselves and her.

"Oh, that is cold," Katie said as spatters hit her face.

"Wawa, wawa!" Magdelene said while throwing water onto Katie's dress.

"Wa-ter," Katie corrected.

"Wawaaa!"

"Wa-ter! Magdelena, say wa-ter!"

A crashing thud caught Katie by surprise and she looked up. Hans, who'd rushed toward the house, collided with one of their boarders. Ulrick stooped over to pick up his scattered schoolbooks and papers.

Katie wished she could run, but not with the bulk she carried. She grabbed her daughter and waddled as fast as she could. "Hans! You must apologize." She shifted Magdelene so she could hold his shoulder, though Hans tried to pull away.

"Ach, you got me wet!" Hans screeched.

"Nevertheless, you must apologize, Hans." She frowned at him. "I have told you to watch where you are going."

Margaret approached from the kitchen. Her chin was tucked and eyebrows raised.

"Ma'am?" Margaret began.

"One moment!" Katie scowled at Hans. "Apologize, now!"

"Forgive me," he mumbled looking at his feet.

"Hans, look him in the eye and say it again!" Katie snapped.

must leave that to Him."

Katie swallowed hard as Elizabeth's pale face flashed into her mind, and she heard the rasping of the child's dying breath. Her pulse sped up and sweat ran down her back. *Oh God, I cannot live through that again.* She sat down and pushed away all the painful thoughts.

"Papa, look at me." Hans made a silly face.

"I saw that." He sat down on a stool by the boy. "Let's play a game. You make a sound, and I shall guess what animal makes that sound."

His eyes aglow, her son nodded. "Oi, oi, oi."

Luther wrinkled his brow and pursed his lips a moment. "That one is hard."

"Listen! I will do it again," Hans said. "Oik, oik, oik."

Magdelene, her big eyes glowing, chimed in to make the sound too, "ooo-eee, ooo-eee."

Her husband slapped the wooden table. "That has to be a horse." He glanced up at Katie and gave her a knowing wink.

Hans howled with laughter, as if he fooled his father. "No, no, no. Papa. It was a pig."

"Oo-ee, oo-ee is pig," Magdelene said, giggling.

He reached over to tweak his daughter's cheek. "That is good, sweetheart. Now, Hans, try another." He pounded the table. "I will guess the next one."

Hans bounced up and down on the rustic bench. "I'll trick you again."

Katie sat down at the table beside her daughter's infant chair. "Say, oink, oink and wrinkle your nose."

"Magdelene wrinkled her nose as directed and made an appropriate sound.

"That was good! Do you want some more cheese?"

Magdelene nodded.

She gave her daughter another helping of cheese and helped herself to bread, cheese, and beer. Even watching the kids play with their father, she still could not extinguish the throbbing in her heart. At last, Katie spoke up. "Doctor Luther, the children should nap after they eat. Would you ask Aunt Lena to put them to bed? I shall check on our visitor now."

He winced. "You and the children will not join us for dinner?"

"They woke so early, I worry they will be irritable and disrupt." She smiled at their sweet faces.

"I understand," he said as he ruffled his son's dark hair. "Very well. When you get older, I want you to dine with us and hear the discussions. Go on, dear. Auntie will help."

She turned her back on the children's laughter and trudged up the stairs to the room where Luther installed her patient. Hilda appeared in the stairwell, and Katie motioned for her to follow. "We have a sick visitor."

Katie hurried to the bed where a girl rested, her clothes tattered. Her childish face was ashen, her skin seared with heat, and her breathing labored. Tears gathered in Katie's eyes as she brushed aside the tangled mass of light brown curls. "She must be thirteen. I had no idea she was so young."

"Is she very ill?" Hilda hovered at Katie's elbow. "Will she need some of your medicines?"

Katie picked up a filthy hand and gazed at her tattered nails. "She is seriously ill. The crisis will come tonight."

"What should we do?" Hilda's green eyes grew wide, as if she were fearful.

Katie looked around the room as she considered the best treatments. "Doctor Luther put her in a convenient room. We have the huge ceramic furnace in the corner. I think we should keep her warm—dehydrate her so her lungs will not fill with water. It is too late for any of my herbal preparations. Build a fire."

Hilda moved toward the door. "Anything else you might need?"

"Bring me some of the evening meal and a blanket. I will stay here all night and make her comfortable. Maybe I can get some sleep in this chair." Katie gestured toward the wooden chair. "And bring me a bucket of water and rags."

"Must you stay here all night?" Hilda asked. Her gaze went from Katie's face to her protruding stomach.

Katie hated to say it. "Yes, I must try to pull her through. That is, if God wills it. Go ahead and get what I need."

"Yes, ma'am!" Hilda hurried from the room.

Alone with her patient, Katie dropped to her knees. As she prayed tears sprang to her eyes. "Oh Father, I should have tended this poor child earlier. I could have delegated any of the tasks I preformed today. My sin could cost this dear child her life. Please help me save her."

She stood and straightened the bedclothes as her stomach knotted. If only God would keep her baby safe.

Hilda made several trips to bring wood, water, blankets, and rags. Katie bathed the girl's face while Hilda built a fire.

"Her skin is very fair, but she has been out in the sun for some time. Her face and neck are sunburned. And she is malnourished." Katie touched her patient's cheek. "I wonder how long she has been on the street. Where are her parents?"

"Does she … have the plague?" Hilda hovered between the door and the furnace, staying a good distance from the bed.

"No, it's an infectious fever. She's been exposed to the elements for some time." She glanced up as Hilda cringed. "Remember that Jesus died for her. Both of us must leave our own health in God's hands."

44

Hilda moved back to the furnace to prod flames that already burned brightly.

"Fetch Fritz. The two of you can bring me enough fuel for the night and fresh water."

Hilda wrung her hands. "Any orders for the household?"

"Margaret knows my plans for dinner. You can help her serve the evening meal. The children will be underfoot, but maybe Aunt Lena will assist you."

Katie turned to her patient with a heavy heart. She bathed the girl in cool water again, but she didn't respond. The child might die regardless of Katie's sacrifice. Should she leave the room and allow the illness to progress? What a terrible thought.

She is so sick. Give me strength for the long night, Father! She pulled the upright chair close to the bed and eased her body onto the edge.

Fritz arrived and piled firewood in the corner of the room. Hilda brought Katie stew from the kitchen and a large jar of beer to sip through the night.

Katie thought about the servants as they served dinner. She hoped they remembered all she taught them.

Through the night, she changed the position of the girl's body and fluffed pillows while she prayed. The sun sank and Katie had to light a lantern. The students usually sat for hours and asked questions after supper. They referred to their discussions as table talk and many wrote down her husband's words. She'd rather be there with him, listening and learning.

Focus on your patient, Katie

As darkness filled the room, Katie stayed alert. She added fuel to the fire often to keep the room warm. Every hour or so, she bathed the girl's face and hands with cool water. "Dear child, God loves you. Please get well."

Katie took her hand. "This is my husband. He wants to pray for you."

Her gaze met Katie's for a moment, as if seeking reassurance. Katie nodded and Maria smiled. "Yes, thank you."

Luther knelt by the bed. "Dear God, thank you for preserving Maria's life. Please help us minister to her soul."

After the prayer, Maria bit her lip. "May … I ask a question?"

Luther rose to his feet. "Aye, child, what do you want?"

"Why did she care for me wh-when she is pregnant? She could get what I have."

A deep crease appeared between Luther's dark brows. "God gives life, and you are valuable to Him. I am leaving my wife in His hands. I hope we can show you the love of God."

Maria gaped first at Luther and then at Katie with a question in her eyes.

"Go back to sleep, dear," Katie said. "We will make sure you are safe."

Luther turned to Katie. "Ach, my little rib, come with me for breakfast. I knew Doctor Katie was the girl's best hope last night. But I think Hilda can handle the nursing from here. She put the new student in Chuck's room because he went to visit his mother."

"Good!" Katie turned her head and rubbed the sore muscles in her shoulders. "I must go down and devise something for dinner." Her stomach swirled.

"Oh, I forgot! Prince John brought several pheasants and some venison by after dinner last night. I told Margaret to prepare it for today."

Katie smiled. *Dear God, you answered my prayer before I even prayed. I should not have worried. We live because you provide all we need.*

She and her husband left the room arm in arm.

48

Contagion

Epilogue

Katie's widowed father took her to a convent when he married his second wife, and Katie took her vows early. Later, she read Luther's writings and decided she wanted her freedom. She and eleven other nuns escaped the convent together.

Her excellent education served her well as the reformer's wife. Dr. Luther often referred to his wife as Katherine von Bora, but he addressed her as Katie

Katie Luther operated a boarding house and several farms. Her keen mind and good business sense made her husband a wealthy man. Their home provided a wonderful outlet for ministry. After supper her husband talked to the students for hours. Years after his death, students printed their conversations—Table Talk.

Chapter Four

Starting Again

Katie Luther wife of Martin Luther
Germany after the Schmalkaldic War
1547

After Martin Luther died in 1546, lawmakers followed out-dated
Saxon laws and assigned guardians to his wife, ignoring the contents
of Luther's will. Katie returned to Wittenberg after the war ended and
discovered numerous barriers to reestablishing her boarding house.

* * *

A stab of pain sliced through Katie Luther's stomach and emptiness echoed in her soul. Yes, she came home. Last night she slept
in her old bed at the Black Cloister, but her dear husband no longer
occupied the other side of the bed. A lifetime of images flooded back.

At least she returned.

Under normal conditions, she pushed aside sorrow to plan her
day. This morning her body didn't want to move. Wouldn't death
be better than this emptiness? Her husband would deplore such

thoughts, and she should also.

Birds outside twilled their songs, and Katie thanked God for their beautiful sound. The rising sun trickled through the slats of the shutters, but shadows still cloaked the simple furnishings. Doctor Luther should be in this room they'd shared for so many years. There stood the straight chair where he'd donned his shoes. The thin cushions looked worn, even sad. The blue and white pitcher where he shaved still stood on the rustic chest. The white crocheted runner hanging over the sides had a grayish cast—much like her heart.

What were the children doing? Were they up yet? They arrived after dark, and she'd best examine the building for damage and start everyone on chores. Perhaps they'd sleep late after the long trip.

If only she could shake this melancholia. Shouldn't she be grateful for God's protection? Charles V did not subdue the Protestant movement. The Black Cloister seemed untouched by the fighting. Now she could reestablish her boarding house and provide for her family.

I have much to do.

The July morning was comfortable. Katie pushed away the thin sheet and sat up, putting her feet on the dark wood. Her floor. After so many years, her feet recognized every crack and crevice. She trudged to the window to fling open the shutters.

Morning sun flooded the room as Katie hurried to the chest to wash. If only she could rinse away the gnawing in her soul, but Christ must be her focus. She took down her braids and ran a brush through her hair before attaching the snood she wore during the day. A glance in the mirror revealed her heart-shaped face was clean and her gray-streaked hair looked fine.

Katie turned, ready to pose a question, but stopped. Doctor Luther lives with the Savior now. Why did she expect him? She knelt and buried her face in the bed covers as tears cascaded from her

know how much freedom your brother gave me. I can be trusted."

He wrapped a lanky arm about her shoulders. "He did a wonderful job caring for you. But now I have that responsibility. You must consult with me."

The hair on the back of her neck stood up. How could Jacob smell like his brother? She must take care how she answered. "I did plan to consult, but I did not want to lose the opportunity. Schnell's grain is particularly fine."

"I do hope you plan to make and sell your beer." He winked at her. "No one else can make it as well anywhere in Germany."

She licked her lips. "Thank you, Jacob. In fact, I do intend to sell beer again, but I must have grain to do that. I also plan on restocking the farms with animals."

His jolly expression collapsed into a frown. "Oh, but that would far exceed your income. I fear you must be cautious."

Didn't he believe she could earn enough to cover her expenses? Doctor Luther knew she could. She wiped a sweaty hand on her skirt. "I certainly shall discuss this with you anon. Right now, I must complete my shopping and get a meal prepared for the children."

"Kiss all of them for me, Katie. Get busy and feed those young ones." He waved as he retreated. "Tell the children I shall visit soon."

If only she could do without guardians. And this was only one of them.

"Katie? Katie Luther."

Doctor Ratzenberger, approached from her left. He was her cousin on her father's side. He assisted her husband with his research and served as medical advisor to the former duke. Ratzenberger was also another one of her guardians. Luther trusted him. Would he be more reasonable? "Hello, Matthew. What a pleasure!"

A smile graced his heart-shaped face. He hoisted her into a crushing embrace. Then he held her at arm's length and looked her up and down. "How are you?"

"I'm a bit on the melancholy side this morning. It's odd, but once I got home, I kept expecting my husband to be here too."

The wind tousled his gray hair. "You've been gone awhile, and that's quite normal."

"Somehow I associate the war with Luther's death, even though it was several months before it broke out. It's as if the world came apart."

"Yours did, Cousin."

She swallowed back tears.

"I understood you returned. I am most pleased you arrived safely."

"Actually we arrived in the wee hours and collapsed into our beds." She gestured toward the Black Cloister. "Today I need to buy enough to feed everyone."

He raised his craggy eyebrows. "I hope you plan on bringing in boarders again?"

"Indeed, I do." Katie smiled. "And I want to sell beer again."

"You do make fine beer, Katie." He put one hand on her shoulder. "I would love to drink some again, but in the absence of your husband, be careful not to take on too much. As your guardian, I think Luther beer should be a thing of the past. In fact, you probably ought to find a smaller house that would cost less to maintain."

Katie sighed and threw up her hands. "A smaller house would not work. I need room for students to board."

A deep frown creased his brow, and he stepped back. "My concern is for you, Katie. You know how much I respected your husband. And you are family. A woman can get in over her head when it comes to business."

Katie leaned toward him and wagged a finger in his face. "Matthew! You know my husband trusted me. He studied, and I did the business. All he ever did was sign papers when I purchased land."

"Do not discount your husband's influence. Doctor Luther had the wisdom to make the sweeping changes required. Germans knew they could follow him. I believe that dreadful war could have been avoided. No, I think you should scale back your activities. Widows do not run businesses."

She put a hand on her hip. "No, no, no! Widows need income. I must feed my children. If I sit at home, we shall all starve."

"Do not discount the memory of the people of Wittenberg, dear cousin," he said with a frown. "They would not allow you to starve."

"Frau Luther! Frau Luther!" Rosalinde, Katie's former maid, yelled and waved.

"Dearest Rosalinde, it's good to see you. Do recall my cousin, Doctor Ratzenberger?"

"Indeed I do. Good day, Doctor." She curtsied.

"Matthew, this is Rosalinde. I took her in as an orphan and trained her to work for me. She can get more done in a day than the average woman."

"Ah. Good day. I seem to remember your face," he said, squinting. He turned back to his cousin. "Katie, I must see to my patients. We will talk again soon."

She turned to her former maid. How fotrunate to find her so soon. "My dear, how are you? When did you return?"

"I came back with the Cranachs in the spring."

Katie's heart warmed. The Cranachs and Luthers had been good friends for years. Lucas Cranach had painted an altar piece to her husband's specifications and portraits of Katie and Luther. His wife, Barbara, had offered to take Rosalinde when Katie left. Barbara knew Katie would have all her children to provide for during the war. "I am so glad that you're safe. Do you want your old job back? I intend to reopen the boarding house.."

Rosaline's gray-green eyes widened. "Frau Luther! Are you sure you want to do that without the good doctor?"

Katie's eyebrows shot up. "Why not?"

Rosalinde's fair skin seemed to pale. "You failed to see what happened after Easter. It gave me quite a turn."

"Well, tell me."

She leaned toward Katie."Twas so dreadful. The Protestants lost Wittenberg, and Emperor Charles rode into town—the very man who made Doctor Luther an outlaw. The old pig was puffed up with pride."

"Yes, I can imagine. He came to Wittenberg after Doctor Luther died."

Rosalinde grabbed Katie's arm. "Folks said he wanted to exhume Doctor Luther and hang him in the square, not that he did. Duke Maurice signed an agreement with him in order to rule the province."

Katie's stomach clenched. "I haven't heard that news."

"Now he must obey a Catholic." She blinked fast. "None of us will be safe. And I hate to think what the emperor would do to you, Frau Luther, if you bring in boarders."

Heat flared in Katie's face and neck. "I refuse to let the emperor or anyone else dictate to me. Charles the thousandth won't stop me. My faith is in Jesus, and I'm going to provide for my family."

Rosalinde's mouth opened.

"Do you want a job?"

"Yes!"

"Then come with me." She tugged Rosalinde's arm and headed home. "I have provisions, now we must get the Black Cloister in shape."

* * *

Katie's fingernails cut into her palms as she knotted her fists. Her boys stood before her, avoiding her gaze. If only they would obey. How did one motivate their children? "Margarete tells me you boys didn't get much done."

Anyone could see that.

"I hoped that you three would work with your sister to get the house in better shape." She glanced around the table at their faces. "It's very important to bring in money, and we need boarders to do that."

Margarete nodded. "It shouldn't take long. All the rooms are dusty, but nothing sustained damage."

Katie nodded. "Your father's friend, Wolf Seibold, agreed to keep an eye on things. We can be thankful for God's protection."

Johann waved toward the front door. "One of my friends came to visit. You recall what father used to say. We must entertain. So we went out back and fought with Catholics."

"Yes. Your father did encourage us to love people." Katie sighed. What an excuse to avoid the work she assigned. "However, my goals take priority at the moment, Johann."

Paul nudged Martin. "He played marbles while I dusted father's books."

"I appreciate that, Paul." Katie gave him a smile. "After lunch we've a lot more of that to do."

Rosalinde entered the room "Excuse me, ma'am. Your brother just arrived."

Hans walked in and nodded, and a lock of his thick brown hair flopped on his brow.

Katie gasped and ran to him. "Hans. I didn't expect you. It's so good to see you."

His tall, lanky frame swallowed Katie in a warm embrace. "Katie, I heard you came home, and I had to come by and see how the family fares."

She pulled away from his arms and waved him join them. "There should be another stool under the table."

"Not yet. I must embrace each of the children," He went round to give each a hug and kiss.

At last Hans settled onto a stool and accepted a wooden plate from Rosalinde.

"Martin, pass him the cheese, and Johann, the cider." Katie hadn't heard from him during the war and she'd worried he'd come to harm. Now as she gazed at him, her heart drifted up to the clouds. "You spoke of my safe return, Brother. I am not so sure that I am safe."

A frown creased his clean-shaven, face. "What do you mean?"

"I want to re-establish our boarding house and sell beer," she said, frowning. "Today I met two of my four guardians. If I obey them, I shall be able to do nothing."

He reached for a slice of cheese. "Remember I act as one of your guardians too. Tell me what they said."

She ticked off their opinions on her fingers. "Jacob does not want me to have a boarding house, but he wants me to sell beer. Matthew thinks I should not sell beer, but he wants me to have boarders—in a smaller house. Both of them fear I am unable to manage without masculine oversight."

"What about mayor?" Margarete said. "Isn't he one of the guardians too?"

"Yes." Katie looked toward the ceiling. "How can I get anything done?"

A mischievous smile crept over her brother's face. "Well, you did not ask me if you should come back. So, I say you should not even be here."

Katie let out a tiny yelp, reached across the table, and gave her brother's hand a playful slap. "I will take off a layer of hide."

Hans winced and sank down. "Aye, she could do it too, children. You must do what she says."

"Hans, I am serious." Katie shook her head. "Luther did not

intend me to have guardians. He also wanted me to be in charge of the children. I have not even spoken to the children's guardians. I shall spend all my time meeting with men who want to guide me. What am I to do? I need no guidance."

Hans choked on his cider.

"Hans? Hans? Are you all right?" She rushed around the table to pound his back. But coughing mixed with laughter? What was going on?

"I-I … am … fine!" He blotted his mouth. "That's enough."

Katie stopped pounding on his back. "Hans, are you laughing?"

He nodded and ducked his head.

Hans had a knack for seeing humor anywhere. But what was funny in this situation? Getting her guardians to agree? The fact that she hadn't talked to those overseeing the children?

A smile tugged at Johann's face. Paul sucked in his cheeks, as if worried about controlling himself. Margarete had her hand over her mouth as if holding in her laughter. Martin pressed his lips together.

Was it funny to everyone but her? "Is everyone finished eating?"

No one spoke, but Hans continued coughing between chuckles.

"Children, go! You all have work to do. Hans and I must talk."

Without a word, her offspring fled, and she sank down on a stool beside Hans and waited for him to recover. He rubbed his huge hands together. "Ach! That is much better. I can breathe again."

"What is the joke?" Katie said.

He took her small hand in his large one. "Sister, you must see the humor. You are complaining about not having freedom. Yet you have more freedom as a widow than any woman in Germany."

She bowed her head and looked at the floor a long time. In a tiny voice she said, "How do other widows survive?"

"Many of them are destitute. Some live with their families. Because you are Katie Luther, you can have a farm and sell beer."

"My husband would deplore the status of widows." She crossed her arms, hugging herself. "He thought women should be educated so they could provide for themselves."

Hans let go of her hand and tapped the table for emphasis. "Your husband changed the world. But a lot more needs to be done."

Tears sprang to her eyes. "I wish he were still here. The world needs him."

"Katie, think about what you said. God took him home."

She shook her head while she wiped away tears. "I know! That was a mistake. I feel like the world needs him."

Hans put his arm around her. "Your husband's job is completed. Now you are alone and must depend on Jesus."

She sniffled. "I do!"

"I have an idea." Hans grinned. "I could gather all of your guardians together. Maybe with all of them in one room, I could convince them of what you want to do."

"Oh, that would help." Her hand went to her chest. "While you work on getting them together, I will go to all three of the farms and get them back in shape. I think Rosalinde can settle any boarders that might come while I am gone. Once I advertise for renters, I should get plenty of interest."

"Oh, Katie." Hans chuckled. "I shall have a bigger job than you."

"Why?"

"Because I shall have to plead for permission when I know you will have the jobs already completed. I have to succeed."

She looked into his dark eyes and laughed.

* * *

Two months later

Katie carried a bouquet of fall flowers into the castle church. She strolled down front and stopped at the stone over her husband's grave. Red, blue, and yellow light filtered from the stained glass windows across the marker at her feet. "Doctor Luther, I miss you."

She wiped a tear away. If only she could talk to him. She'd tell him she came back after the war and set up the boarding house, and she sold beer in the town square again. Several guardians tried to help, even though she didn't need it. Despite all the ups and downs of life, God provided everything she needed.

"I have frustrating days, but we had those while you lived. Someday I shall meet you again in heaven. Until then, I know God won't forsake me. I love you."

She placed the flowers on his grave and went back into the fall sunshine tearful, yet smiling.

Epilogue

Katie Luther maintained her boarding house until 1552, when a plague forced university officials to relocate the school in Torgau. She fled the city with her two youngest children. After suffering an accident at Torgau, she died at the age of 53. Her family erected a monument in the Torgau church where she is buried.

Chapter Five

The Price of Freedom

Duchess Louise

1824

Coburg, Germany

When Duchess Louise discovered her husband's evil habits, her romantic infatuation dissolved into disgust. His flirtations embarrassed and annoyed her. Can she break free of her horrible life and find happiness again?

* * *

Shuddering, Duchess Louise glanced down at the rushing water below her in the River Itz. Did she dare to leap off the balcony into the swirling stream? She preferred action, and this would stop the ache. The rocks beneath the surface would bring oblivion. If only she could be more attractive or more intelligent. She tried to please Ernst, but she failed.

But why should she suffer such a death? Unlike the Duke, she had no guilt. Besides, she hated pain, and she refused to inflict that

months. I cannot say why he finally consented. Now I understand his concern. He caught a whiff of the man's reputation."

The soldier said nothing.

"I had warning." She held out a rumpled paper. "This letter came to me, unsigned. How it unnerved me. The writer made ... disagreeable accusations. I shared them with my childhood playmate, but I feared telling my father. He would scold me for listening to gossip."

"Your Grace, I am not sure how I can assist you."

She stood and ambled toward the railing. "This morning I thought of tossing myself off into the water below. Would it be quick? I don't know."

"No!" The soldier strode toward her and blocked her from the railing. "That will solve nothing."

"You think I overreact?" She turned aside. "You trust the Duke because he parrots Luther's words? The Duke's words mean nothing. He intends to deceive."

"I see." The man's face hardened.

The Duchess clasped her hands at her waist. "After we married, I heard gossip, but I looked into his engaging eyes and refused to believe. Only after I had my second son did I see the outrageous flirting. Now I fear him."

The soldier's face darkened and a muscle twitched in his temple.

"Recently I made a slight reference to his activities, and he twisted my arm behind my back until I cried out in pain." How unpleasant to reveal such dreadful secrets. What must the man think of her? But she must press on. "The bruises lasted a week."

The young man knelt before her and said, "I offer my assistance."

"I knew you would listen," she said with a sigh. "My case is a sad one, but with your help, I might hope. Ernst refused to give me a divorce. My plan will not be easy, but I shall ask you to commit no crime."

He raised his head, narrowing his eyes. "I understand. But what duty shall I perform?"

Louise clutched her small hands in her lap. Her grip turned them white. If only she could find another way. "I shall flirt with you at court. That is all. I hope to create a spectacle so I can have a divorce."

"But surely, Ma'am, this endangers you." His brow crinkled. "If he leans toward violence—"

"I can contrive nothing better." She shook her head. "Can you?"

"If I could have time to consider—"

"What are your duties?"

"I am in charge of a battalion of men based at the Veste, and I manage the security at the castle in Coburg."

She closed her eyes and nodded. "I shall request your presence for any court event I must attend and bring security matters to your attention. Treat me with cordial respect, nothing else. I simply could not do such a thing without taking you into my confidence."

He bowed his head. "I understand, Your Grace."

* * *

Louise pushed aside her food. Everything tasted like sand. Afternoon shadows entwined themselves around the room. The dressing table, armoire, and chest stood open and empty, like her heart. Now that she knew the outcome, would she do it all again?

She must gain her freedom.

"Your Grace?"

The Duchess opened her eyes and Letitia stood beside her "Yes?"

"The footman will be here soon for your trunks."

Louise slid to the edge of the bed and stood. But the room spun and she swayed. Letitia wrapped an arm about her waist. "Are you ill, Ma'am?"

"No. No." She must not linger. Her body might be weak, but her determination as hard as stone. "I am fine."

Her maid eased her onto a chair. "I wish you would eat. You lost so much weight, and that dress needs altering again."

"A bit of sleep will cure me."

"No. That is all you do." Letitia shook her head and offered her a sip of water. "You've been through so much."

"My sons cried when I said good bye. They looked so thin and pitiful." Her tongue touched a salty tear that trickled onto her lip.

"Ma'am, they had a simple childhood fever." Her maid grabbed a cloak. "They shall soon recover."

"Yes, but I shall never see them again." Sobs wrenched her body. She regretted her rash choice for the boys' sake. If only she could reverse the past and devise ways to avoid Ernst.

"Oh, Ma'am." The maid patted her shoulder. "I feel sure the Duke will relent."

"Ernst? Never." She handed the glass back. "I cannot bear the horrible lies he spread at the trial."

"Everyone knows who bears the guilt."

"Yet I am to bear the legal shame—adulteress and divorcée." She touched her maid's arm. "Without my loyal Letitia, I would have died."

"It is a pleasure to serve you, Ma'am." She slipped the cloak about Louise's shoulders. "You must forget if you wish to regain your strength. Think of good things now."

"I regret all this for von Hanstein. Neither of us would stoop to immorality."

"I should not worry about him. He's a clever man with friends."

"I am thankful the duke could not obtain my mother's property." She pulled her wrap closer, as if it could protect her.

Another maid, Alice, burst into the room. Her eyes were wide, and her face white. "Your Grace … there is a p-p-problem."

"Yes?" Louise sighed and sank back into the chair.

Alice opened and closed her mouth while gesturing toward the front of the house. "The men … they demand you."

Louise shook her head. None of this made sense. Perhaps her poor diet impacted her ability to think. "Men? Which men?"

"Men from the town. You must come."

"The duchess is exhausted," Letitia said. "Tell them she cannot come."

"They are armed." Alice wrung her hands.

Suddenly cold, Louise shuddered. What could this mean? Had Coburg turned against her? She glanced at her maids. Letitia chewed her lip, and Alice twisted a lock of her hair. The men might get violent, and Louise wanted the servants safe. "I feel fine now, Letitia, I shall go."

"But Ma'am …" Letitia frowned.

Alice scampered downstairs.

"I don't want them to harm anyone." Louise kept a measured pace down the spiral staircase. Alice kept looking back with a frown, as if worried by her lack of speed. Was she making a mistake? What could she say to calm an angry crowd?

The huge front door stood open. A mob of men congregated outside the doorway. Louise's heart staggered about in her chest as she scanned their rifles and solemn faces. She stepped back.

"Duchess Louise, come to the carriage," several men called. "Duchess!"

"Your Grace, we want to take you back."

"We would not hurt you, Ma'am."

She took a tentative step forward, and men fell to their knees.

Trembling, she forced a smile and looked at the mass of kneeling men. "How may I help you? Do you need something?"

The men slowly stood, and a murmur went through the crowd.

Her heart hammered against her ribs, but she kept smiling. "I

69

see guns, and they make me fear you. What do you want?"

An older man with a full, gray beard spoke up, "You have no need to fear. You must return to Coburg. We will take you."

A man from the middle of the group yelled, "Marriage is for life. We must reconcile you with the Duke."

A young boy from the right side yelled, "You belong to us, and we love you. We hope the Duke will see that."

She took a deep breath and said, "I need my trunks. Give me three strong men, without guns, to fetch my bags."

Several men stepped up.

She pointed toward three and waved them toward Alice. "Show them the way, Alice."

Letitia hovered behind her. She turned back to the crowd, and the men parted ranks, making a path to the carriage.

"I want my maid, Letitia," she said.

A bearded man with dark brown hair stood at the open door. "Yes, Ma'am. She may come too."

"Very well, I am ready." Nodding and smiling at the men, she walked forward. The dark-headed man offered a calloused hand at the carriage door. She put her small trembling hand into his, and he assisted her inside. She leaned back on the upholstered cushions and sighed. What now?

The horses whinnied as she gazed outside. Men unhooked them and fastened themselves in front of the carriage.

They are going to lug me all the way?

A male voice shouted. "Let's heave together now! Pull!"

The carriage inched along, heaved by the men. Darkness fell, and the sea of faces faded into the shadows. But the murmur of their voices mingled with the sounds of their feet and the moans of the men who shared the load.

Oh God, please keep me safe. These armed peasants seem to

believe in me, but they may not understand the Duke's determination.

At last, the carriage came to a halt, and a cheer reverberated through the night. The door opened, and the dark-haired man once more offered his hand. After she alighted from the carriage, he took her arm. Flanked by two armed men, he led her to the doorway of Ehrenburg, the Duke's Coburg palace. Her maid followed behind.

Several men with guns preceded him and knocked. A servant, who held a lighted candelabrum, opened the door.

The men shouted, "We present the Duchess of Coburg! We present the Duchess of Coburg."

Louise's muscles quivered as her escort released her, and she walked in. The same three men followed her with trunks and deposited them in the hallway.

In a hoarse tone, the butler asked, "Your Grace, where do you want your trunks?"

"Put them in the fourth guest room on the third floor."

He bowed. "Yes, Ma'am."

Letitia removed Louise's cloak and handed it to the butler.

Louise's legs wobbled about like pudding as she collapsed into a chair in the Duke's receiving room. Letitia entered behind her and lit a few candles to extinguish the darkness. "Isn't that better?"

"Yes, thank you. I never thought I would ever see this room again."

"The men told me they are bringing the Duke here, too," Letitia whispered.

Louise gasped. "Oh, no!"

The maid leaned close and whispered, "They want to reunite you."

"I thought I never had to see Ernst again."

"Hello, Louise," Ernst said as he strode in. Dark curls framed his scowling face. "All of this is your fault. Coburg is about to riot, woman—because of you."

She clasped her hands and rose to face him, "What was I supposed to do, ignore your escapades? I grew tired of your pious speeches about honor and avid devotion to Luther's words. You have Coburg deceived, but not me."

A vein throbbed in his temple. He grabbed her arm and twisted it behind her back. "Ouch!"

"Yes. Women should ignore certain things, but you failed to."

"Let me go." Tears came to her eyes.

He leaned his face close to hers, and his lip curled. "I have tried for years to find true love. When I saw your face, I thought I had. But you were unable to make intelligent conversation. How could you satisfy me? My mind is so far above yours."

His words burned into the brokenness of her soul. If only she could run from the room and stop up her ears. "Do you plan to tell the citizens outside? They will not let you hurt me."

"I will tell you what you must do, dearest. You will walk with me out on the balcony and smile and wave to the men like everything is fine between us."

His breath on her face brought waves of nausea. "No, I will not pretend."

He twisted her arm a little more.

"Ouch—please stop!"

"I shall." His grip tightened. "If you promise to wave to the crowd."

"I promise, just let me go,"

He loosed his grip on her arm. "Very well, but if you refuse, I will break your arm."

"I hate you, Ernst. I shall file charges."

He laughed. "Who would convict me? I hire the judges."

She looked at the huge red mark and massaged her arm. Once more he goaded her into saying things she despised. Why couldn't she maintain her poise around him?

"Are you ready, dearest? We must calm the crowd now." He

held out his arm to her.

Louise gagged and inhaled to quell the nausea. What a terrible moment to vomit. Must she touch him again? "I need a moment."

"What's wrong, honey?" A sneer twisted his thin lips. "You're a wonderful actress. You had me convinced of your steadfast love."

Why didn't he stab her? That would hurt less. She offered him complete devotion until she learned the depths of his evil. Louise stamped her foot. "I did love you."

"See," he said, pointing a long, thin finger into her face. "I could look into your eyes and imagine you are truthful."

She lifted her chin, determined to do what it took to escape his control. "I am ready."

Swallowing hard, she put a hand on his arm, and together they strode to the French doors. Servants opened the doors wide. Together, Louise and Duke Ernst stepped onto the balcony. In the darkness she made out a mass of faces. A hurrah went up. Ernst waved and smiled.

Louise gulped and smiled too. She raised a hand to wave. Would this please Ernst? How often she tried in the past, to no avail. Why did she long for that so much? Suddenly the crowd burst into a hymn. The men sang every verse. Louise filled her lungs and kept a smile on her face, despite the churning in her stomach.

The Duke raised his hand. "I know how strongly you feel about maintaining family ties. The great reformer would agree!"

The crowd cheered. The duke smiled and waved, and Louise followed his lead. At last the Duke took her arm and guided her back inside.

"They did not disperse. Yet, they seem happy." She dropped into a chair.

"Von Hanstein would be able to handle them. He is no longer here, thanks to you."

She frowned. "But they do not seem violent now." Louise shrank from his hardened face.

"Go to your room. A messenger will notify you when it is safe to leave. I might have to call the military."

She fled to the guest room.

* * *

Fall 1826

Louise sighed. She imagined a handsome man who professed his love. He whisked her away on his horse and galloped across the field far from her enemies. He had an arm about her waist, and the pressure was comforting. She wore silks again, and expensive riding boots.

A maid in a starched white uniform entered. "Madam?"

The vision faded, and she sat once more in her small home in St. Wendel, staring at an open field. If only she could find someone to love her. "Yes?"

"Count Polzig requests to see you."

"Who?" Louise brushed invisible debris from her clothing and grabbed a pen to appear busy. "I suppose I should see him. It's better than sitting here alone."

Moments later, a man walked in wearing a dark tailcoat, beige silk waist coat over a white shirt, black cravat, and white slacks. "Your Grace, or should I call you Louise?"

Louise dropped her pen. "But she called you—"

"Count Polzig. That is my title." A huge smile dominated his face.

She stood up and giggled while she gazed into his deep green eyes. "Von Hanstein, how did you get a title?"

His green eyes twinkled. "The duke reigns supreme over a very small German province. He does not deceive men outside his jurisdiction. Duke Frederick of Saxe-Hildburghausen bestowed the title on me, but the King of Prussia holds me in high regard as well."

"After the trial, I wondered. The men who gave evidence made

Ernst look wonderful, and they told wicked tales about me."

He raised a sandy eyebrow. "Those men work for the duke. They had to exaggerate to accomplish what he wanted. He wanted to be free of you and keep your father's province."

A lighthearted chuckle escaped. "I wondered if all Coburg hated me. But I didn't know what to make of the peasants who escorted me to Ehrenburg. They were polite, despite their guns."

"Those peasants knew Duke Ernst. They brought weapons to protect themselves." He pointed at her. "They loved you."

She tucked her chin. "They were so polite, and I sensed they cared. I don't think Ernst ever did. Is it possible Ernst married me to get my father's lands?"

Von Hanstein grimaced. "Everyone knows how much the duke loves hunting.

"It hurts to know he used me." Louise closed her eyes and bit her lip.

"He is a wealthy man who can surround himself with comforts."

The count spread his hands. "He has the ability to get what he wants—even if it is unjust."

"Unjust!" She looked at the ceiling. "I cried for days when I heard he relieved you of your duties. I know you did nothing."

I knew the risks, Ma'am." He stepped closer. "I never touched you, but I must admit guilt."

Her blue eyes widened. "Guilt? For what?"

He bowed his head for a moment. "I fell in love with you."

Warmth filled her cheeks. "Ah! I did see something in your eyes. But as a married woman, I could not hope."

"You could not hope then." He placed a kiss on her small hand. "But what about now?"

She closed her eyes and shuddered. "Now? Now? I am a divorced woman—accused of adultery."

Chapter Six

A Better Man

SusannahThompson, fiancé of C.H. Spurgeon
England
Circa 1855

Susannah Thompson always wanted a story book romance but never dreamed she'd attract C.H. Spurgeon. As an upper class lady, she perfected her manners and expected no less from him. After all, he earned the respect of thousands. But what if he failed? Could she find a way to love a godly man who wasn't perfect?

* * *

Ouch! Someone ran into Susannah as she and Charles entered the Horns. Men, dressed in dark suits and ladies in sweeping skirts elbowed past her into the lecture hall. She looked about, but no one met her gaze. They didn't know her, and she preferred that despite her illustrious fiancé.

Charles kept moving forward, and she almost lost her grip on his arm.

The foyer doors stood open behind her, and the breeze rustled the ladies bonnets and whisked amongst the bareheaded men. Their faces were tight, anxious. If only she were already seated inside.

Light from gas chandeliers overhead mingled with the rays of the setting sun. The building was quite pretty, or at least the part she could see. The swarm blocked her view. She leaned close to Charles. "Are all these people coming to hear you?"

He shrugged and spoke in her ear. "If they are, I shall have quite an audience today."

"What a wonderful opportunity to reach the lost." The multitude almost pulled them apart, and Charles didn't respond. She raised her voice over the clatter. "How much further?"

"It's just up those stairs," He pulled her closer and guided her toward the stairway ahead.

At last they ascended the carpeted stairs one-by-one. Her stomach reeled as people pressed in, and she almost stumbled. She grasped the engraved handrail while she clutched Charles with her other hand. If only she could arrive without an embarrassing tumble.

Susannah's beaded purse caught in the vertical wood railings. She tugged it loose and examined it for a second but nothing appeared damaged. She reached for her intended, but her hand landed on a woman dressed in green muslin.

The lady frowned and moved away.

"Charles? Charles?"

The back of his head bobbed above several people between them as he climbed higher.

She forced herself onto the next step, trying to get close. "I am back here."

He moved further away.

Surely he must know she was no longer beside him. "Charles!"

His head disappeared in the mob. The room spun as the people continued to swell forward.

She clenched her teeth and pushed up several more steps to the landing. But once on level ground people compressed even tighter about Susannah. She inched her way to the wall and leaned against the dark paneling. The pungent smells of body odor and perfume permeated the air. Perspiration broke out on her face, so she untied her cloak and draped it on her arm. She glanced at her gold watch pinned to her dress. The service did not commence for thirty-five minutes and already the place was packed.

Her gaze caught a young couple on the edge of the crowd. The attractive lady, resplendent in a scarlet and gold dress with a matching cape, clung to the man's arm, and her gray eyes twinkled as she talked to him. The man lifted her gloved hand to his mouth giving it a prolonged kiss as they moved forward toward the balcony door.

She sighed at the sweetness. The man displayed the perfect attitude without being overbearing or syrupy. Memories of Charles smiling into her face flashed into her mind. Under most circumstance, he overflowed with affection. She smiled at the memory of him kissing her hand the first time. He would return for her. Soon. A man with such a fine reputation would not leave her to battle the crowd.

But the minutes ticked by. Ten … fifteen. The surging crowds made her shrink further into the wall so that she could hardly breathe. Sweat broke out on her forehead and she dabbed away the moisture with her lacy handkerchief. If perspiration drenched her clothing, she'd best retreat to the lady's room before he spoke.

Where is Charles? On occasion he arrived late because of his duties, but surely he would not forget her. She would not do the same to him. Never. In fact, she couldn't even bear the thought of letting him down. She surrendered every fiber of her heart to this man and would do anything he needed.

She fingered her watch and stood on tiptoe. If only she had her fan. Her limp handkerchief could hold nothing more. Was it possible that he loved her less than she loved him? He professed undying affection for her. How could he lose her in a crowd? She did not intend to stand there and allow this mob to crush her.

With a huff, she gathered up her skirt and flung herself into the throng, going back to the door. "Excuse me. Pardon me."

Inch-by-inch she forced her way through the dense horde until she reached the stairs. Turning sideways, and apologizing, she fought her way down the steps and to the entrance. She stopped and stared. The throng extended to the cobblestone walkway outside. She did not get free until she'd walked several blocks.

"Whew!" How incredibly rowdy! As she inhaled the crisp breeze, she threw her cloak around her shoulders, and strutted down the walkway.

A picture of Charles' smile flitted into her mind. She paused and looked back at the people entering the Horns Assembly room. He might worry … if he ever realized her absence. Would he? What came over him?

But she mustn't stand around. Reputable women did not wander London streets at this hour.

A hansom, pulled by a black horse, rounded the corner.

Thank Goodness! She ran to the curb and waved.

The driver tipped his hat and pulled on the reins, bringing the vehicle to a stop. "Where to ma'am?"

"Number 7, St. Anne's Terrace, sir. Quickly."

The driver dipped his head. "Yes, ma'am."

She climbed inside and collapsed against the seat. Imaginings of hooligans swam before her eyes and her insides trembled. If only Charles had escorted her to a seat to ensure her safety. His behavior failed to match his sweet letters and charming words—the very thing he preached against. She pressed her fingers against her eyes

"No. I shall talk with him." Mrs. Thompson put down the book of poems she was reading aloud. "Please take him to the sitting room. Susie, he will want to speak with you."

She shrugged and refused to make eye contact. Conflict made her uncomfortable. How she longed for righteousness, and she feared today she'd fallen short. Was it wrong to be hurt? Charles would recognize her anger and no doubt he would not hesitate to point out evil. Which of her feelings were selfish and which were normal?

On the other hand, Mother handled tense situations with incredible tact. Perhaps she could untangle this mess without Susie's input. Will Charles apologize? She imagined him begging her forgiveness. As his fiancé, she deserved a place in his life. But what?

Mrs. Thompson returned with a puckered brow. "Susannah, Charles was quite distressed. It took quite an effort to reassure him. Now he wants to speak to you."

Susie liked the sound of "distressed." Maybe he was truly sorry. How did he look when he was upset? "You say he was anxious? How did he respond when you explained?"

"I merely assured him of your safety."

She couldn't mistake the determined expression on her mother's face. "I have to tell him?"

"Yes, come. I promised you would come straight away." Mrs. Thompson held out her hands.

Susie hung back. What would Charles say? He'd never seen her irate. She hated being scolded, and he might do that.

Mrs. Thompson took her arm. "Come along!"

Susannah obeyed even though her stomach churned as if she walked to her execution. Once she reached the sitting room, Charles paced in front of the window, his shoulders sagging.

He came toward her with his hands extended. "Susie, thank God you are unhurt."

"Good evening." She refused to meet his gaze. Instead she curtsied and moved to the camel back couch on the other side of the room. She settled herself on the brocade cushions and arranged each tier of her flounced skirt.

Spurgeon strode toward her and stood beside a French armchair nearby. "May I sit?"

"Please do." She glanced up to see him frowning, but she returned to her skirt, fingering the pink edging.

He eased himself into the chair, and blotted his face with his handkerchief. "After the sermon, I realized I had not seen you since we entered the building. I waved aside the people who wanted to consult with me and asked the ushers to help search for you. When we found no trace of you, my heart pounded. I ... I was frantic. I feared you came to harm."

So he did miss me—after his sermon. She looked into his face. Lines of fatigue spread around his mouth and eyes. His hair was mussed as if he had run his fingers through it over and over, and his cravat was askew. "I held onto your arm until we reached the steps, but my purse caught in the railing. The crowd pushed forward and you went on without me. I thought ... I thought you would come back for me, but you did not."

Spurgeon tugged at his collar. "So I lost you in the crowd before the service. I had no idea. Quite dreadful!"

"Finally I made it up to the landing, but there the crowd packed in even more tightly. I moved to the wall thinking you would return. I started wondering how you could love me ... and completely forget I existed."

He laced his fingers together and winced. "Please go on."

"After a long wait, I-I lost my temper. I fought the crowd to get out of the building. Even outside, I had to battle people still trying to get in. Fortunately I could afford to hire a cab. Frankly, you dis-

birth to twin boys, Thomas and Charles. For ten years she worked alongside her husband in Metropolitan Tabernacle. From 1868, illness kept her from an active life, yet she maintained a fund that gave books, clothing, and stationery to needy ministers.

She wrote several devotionals and two books on the building fund. After her husband died, she edited the *Sword and Trowel* for several years.

Chapter Seven

A Handful of Peppermint Candy

Ellen McCallie, wife of Pastor Thomas Hooke McCallie
Chattanooga, Tennessee
September 9, 1863

Ellen McCallie wanted to obey God and her husband, but the Union army targeted their city as a gateway to the South. How could she hang onto her faith when her household could face danger?

* * *

Ellen McCallie's stomach knotted. She stood at the sitting room window and inhaled, hoping to achieve calmness. Confederate soldiers marched past, going south. Images of men firing guns flashed in her mind. How would she protect little Mary? At this moment, she'd rather be anywhere but here. War on her doorstep? Unthinkable!

Her husband, Reverend Thomas McCallie, appeared beside her and draped an arm about her shoulders. "It appears they're leaving town."

Ellen focused on keeping an even tone. Their toddler, playing

But she came to support her husband. Today he'd better describe how God punished sinners. With her gaze on the polished hardwood floor, she scurried past them to her usual front-row seat. Once she settled Mary beside her with a cloth doll, Ellen clasped her Bible until her knuckles turned white.

After a few hymns, her husband stood to speak, and sunlight glistened on his sweaty brow.

Don't work so hard for these soldiers, Hon. What a sinful thought to have in church.

Tom opened his Bible. Resolve shone in his eyes. "A war rages in our land. Everyone is divided between the Union and the Confederates."

They didn't favor seceding nor like invaders either. Ellen rearranged her skirt as Mary climbed into her lap. Could she sit still? She usually handled fear with hard work, but not during a service.

"A soldier resides in the heart of each citizen, either in blue or gray. But I ask you to consider a more serious issue. Where would you be if you died today?"

A Union soldier to her left sniffled into his handkerchief. She wanted these men to understand God's message. But her family must leave the city before a battle broke out.

* * *

November 24, 1863,

Dusk

Fire raced through Reverend McCallie's limbs. He put aside sermon preparation in his study. Could the noise outside be the sound of cannon fire? An earthquake seemed unlikely—war raged in the South. If fighting came to the city, he must protect his family. Tom rose from his knees and rushed to the study window but nothing seemed out of place. "Ellen!" He raised his voice. "I'm investigating outdoors. I shall return soon."

Dishtowel in hand, his wife peered through the kitchen door. "Please be careful, Tom."

He nodded. In the hallway, he grabbed a jacket from the coat stand and tromped into the yard, avoiding the tents Union soldiers erected. As he neared the city, the sound grew louder. Soldiers marched in rows of seven or more. Soon they'd be passing his home. Ellen would be worried.

Tom's stomach burned as he turned back to the house. What would Ellen say? Perhaps she could visit with her mother if the battle came too near. "Ellen?" He glanced about the sitting room, but his wife darted about sweeping the kitchen with unusual vigor.

"Easy, Honey." He managed to grab one arm as she scurried past. "If you keep this up I shall have to replace the kitchen floor."

Already a strand of brown hair escaped the tight bun behind her neck. "Tom, you know how I detest filth. I shall tackle the frying pan next."

"Nothing in here is filthy, Ellen." Thomas pulled her into his arms. The muscles in her back and shoulders were rigid under his touch. He massaged the knots. "The battle won't be in Chattanooga."

"Where do you think the soldiers are going?"

If you recall, Confederates still hold the ridge. I suspect the Union intends to take Missionary Ridge. The battle will be several miles away." He released her, and then tilted her face up. Deep lines between her brows betrayed Ellen's fear. "I know you are afraid. I am too. It is uncanny having the battle so close. Remember, God is with us."

Ellen looked down and pulled away. "We can't be sure the battle won't come this way."

"If it does, I shall take all of you to safety."

"How will you know if we must leave?" She tucked strands back into the bun.

He had an answer, but he preferred not to reveal his thoughts at the moment. God would show him. He kept up a silent conversation with the Almighty. "I shall know."

"I'd best make some coffee." She hurried to the stove.

Ellen doesn't appear calmer.

* * *

November 25, 1863

Trying to shut out the sounds outside, Ellen donned a muslin apron to protect her dark blue dress and put on water for coffee. Tom reported cannon fire at Missionary Ridge this morning. Each bang made dishes rattle in her cabinets, which she tried to ignore. Staying busy helped keep her mind off worry, so she picked up the pace again. She bustled across the kitchen and grabbed ingredients for biscuits.

An odd noise came from behind her. She jumped and squealed. Were soldiers about to attack their home? Was her husband mistaken?

She turned and Mary scooted about under the table. "Mary." She let out a ragged breath. "Are you hungry?"

Mary grinned and nodded as she stuck a finger in her mouth.

Lord, help me get past this fear.

"Hello, Mary. Come to Daddy." Tom scooped her up and placed her on his shoulders.

"Go, Dada." Her blue eyes shone.

For a brief second an image of guns pointed toward Tom popped into her mind. She took a deep breath and raced across the room for a dishrag to swab the table.

"You're doing breakfast in record time." Tom winked at her as he galloped about the kitchen with their daughter on his shoulders. He snorted and neighed like a horse. Mary's blond hair bounced as she threw back her head and laughed.

Would her family make it through this battle? Or would they

be dead at the end of the day? What a shame war threatened to end their happy home. Ellen pushed away thoughts of cannon fire. She blotted a tear and kept working.

Father, protect my precious family.

"Tom, you'd best go into the attic today for more flour. I emptied the canister."

"I shall fetch it after breakfast."

If only the secret stash of essentials would last, but the Bible called such thoughts worry. She bit her lip and praised God her husband had the cunning to create such a hiding place.

The enormous explosions continued through their meager breakfast of biscuits and coffee. Last night she'd praised God once the marching ended, but this bothered her more. Men would die today, a few miles from their home.

She finished clearing the breakfast dishes. Mary sat in her grandmother's lap, so Ellen bustled to her husband's study. "Tom, what do you think? Are they about to attack?"

"I'm wondering the same thing. I shall go out and check on the situation." He stood and grabbed his hat. "But I want you to stay here. Do not prepare the soup for the hospital until I return. I think we should deliver it together."

Ellen sighed. "Take care of yourself." Since the Union army occupied Chattanooga, the family stayed indoors most of the time.

He squeezed her hand. "I will stay out of the range of the cannons."

"But you could be hit by a stray bullet. Aren't you afraid?"

"Yes, I am frightened, but I refuse to give way. I believe I am where I should be. I am safer here than anywhere else." He set his jaw and left the room.

Hearing him open and shut the front door, she clasped her hands and squeezed until they hurt.

Ellen finished her morning chores. She put Mary down for a nap

around. My wife and children are back home in Kentucky, and I'd hope someone would help them out if they were hungry. It's not much, but perhaps it will stave off hunger."

Ellen blinked and released a huge sigh. "Thank you, sir. This will come in handy."

He gave a brief smile as he left.

She carried it to the kitchen and dropped to her knees by the table. They'd eaten all their canned vegetables and dried meat. The last few days their meals had been biscuits and coffee. "Dear God, thank you for your provision."

"Ellen?" Her husband stood behind her. His shoulders sagged. "I found nothing to purchase."

"At least you are safe. I couldn't imagine losing you." She walked into his embrace and snuggled her cheek against the roughness of his shirt. He smelled of handmade lye soap. "A Union soldier came a few minutes ago. He gave us some hard tack."

Tom kissed the top of her head. "Praise God, we have something to eat."

"Yes." She suppressed thoughts of the applesauce and vegetables the soldiers took.

Lord, I never thought I'd be thankful for hard tack.

* * *

Christmas Eve

Ellen's throat was tight and her eyes stung. She pulled her hands from the warm dishwater and dabbed her face with a damp towel to hold back tears. Weeping would upset Tom. He did his best to protect them. But she lost the battle and dampness pooled in her eyes, dribbling down her cheeks. Was she a terrible Christian?

Despite her determination to praise God and forget the holiday, her mind kept returning to the past. Her family always decorated the day before Christmas, cooked a special dinner, and sang carols

102

around the fireplace. The jubilation of Christmas seemed so far away. Tonight she served hard tack and coffee. And she was thankful for something to eat, but the hardships of the past six months rankled. She looked down at her the soapy water. It resembled her heart—murky and dark.

Dreadful situation!

She must try.

Why not do something to celebrate the birth of the Savior? After all, the angels performed music for humble shepherds, and they proclaimed the entire world should rejoice. Why should a war keep her from doing something festive? Taking a deep breath, she hustled to her bedroom for a sock and then found a hammer and nails in her husband's toolbox. As she nailed the sock on the mantel, her husband appeared beside her. His bushy brows pulled together.

"What are you doing, Ellen?"

"I am putting up a stocking," She looked him in the eye. "War or not, this is Christmas Eve."

Tom ran a hand over his face. "That's fine, Honey. Go on to bed. I think I shall study a bit before I retire."

"Good night, then, Dear." She nodded as she left the room.

* * *

Tom listened. His wife proceeded down the hall and up the steps. Satisfied she'd entered the bedroom, he waited ten minutes longer. Then he tiptoed into the kitchen, and lit a small lantern. He donned his heavy coat and slipped out into the cold evening.

The icy wind whipped his face and flakes of snow swirled around him. He shivered. "Father, I know you care about our smallest concerns. Help me to find a special gift for Ellen's stocking."

He lifted the lantern high. Proceeding with care around the soldier's tents, he made his way to the road. The darkened city loomed before him. Several small campfires, surrounded by more tents, sat on the edge of the city. A few remaining occupied homes in the city had lights in the windows. Going down the main road, he headed toward the Tennessee River. Since supplies and merchants would arrive on the river, his best chance of finding what he wanted would be there. After walking several miles, a figure came out of the darkness and blocked the path.

"It's a cold night, sir."

Tom could not see his face, but could discern the outline of his clothes. He was surely an officer. "Yes sir, it is. But since it's Christmas Eve, I'm looking for a gift for my wife."

"You are not a soldier, are you?"

"I am Reverend McCallie."

"Oh, yes! You're the minister we called before the execution last week."

"Yes." Tom tensed at the memory of the condemned young man.

"Did the man—make his peace with God?"

"I wish I could answer yes. I gave him every chance, but I do not think so." Tom replied.

"You did what you could. Now tell me, what are you hoping to find?" The officer's voice had softened.

"My wife, Ellen, insisted on hanging a stocking. I hoped to find a merchant who would sell me a small gift to drop inside."

The soldier nodded and motioned for Tom to follow. "I can help you there. A sutler came into town this afternoon. He asked permission to sell to the soldiers. I will take you to him."

The two men walked in silence for several blocks. Then they came upon a small cabin with light streaming from the window. Lamplight fell across the officer's stripes. A major.

The officer knocked on the cabin door. In a moment, a heavy man with a round face opened the door.

"I have a customer for you," the officer said, gesturing toward Tom.

"Yes, sir. Please come in." He waved them indoors. "As you can see, I came from Florida with a fine selection of fruit and several kinds of candy."

As soon as Tom stepped inside the cabin, he smelled oranges. Once his eyes adjusted to the light, he could see that crates of fruit filled the small room. "How much are the oranges?"

"Two for fifty cents," the man said.

The major shook his graying head. "That seems expensive."

The merchant flinched and cleared his throat. "I will give you three for fifty cents and throw in a handful of peppermint candies too."

Tom smiled and reached into his pocket. "It is a deal." He handed the merchant the money. After receiving the fruit and candy, he filled his coat pockets.

Once he completed the transaction, the two men walked out. Tom turned to the major. "I want to thank you for your kindness. My wife will be thrilled about the fruit, and I never expected to get candy."

The major shook his head. "No sir, I need to thank you. You stayed here and risked your life to minister to these men. I consider it a pleasure to do something for you. Merry Christmas."

"I plan to have services in my home, once stability returns. I would be pleased if you would come," Tom said.

"I should enjoy attending church again. Thank you!"

The men parted with a handshake, and Tom went home. Chuckling with joy, he unloaded his pockets into the stocking. The sight of the bulging stocking brought a smile. "Thank you. I'm amazed at your goodness. You answered even before I prayed." He returned his coat and the lantern to the kitchen and then climbed the stairs to bed.

He stooped to kiss Ellen's cheek. Her cheek and her pillow were damp.

Oh, Ellen. I have a surprise for you.

He climbed into bed and drifted off.

* * *

A shrill cry woke Tom the next morning. Throwing on his robe, he ran to the sitting room.

Ellen stood before the fireplace, her eyes sparkling. "Husband, where did you find these? Oranges! And peppermint candy is my favorite."

He put his arms around her. "The Lord always provides, Ellen. Merry Christmas."

Tears flowed down her face. "God is so good. I know we are right where he wants us."

Epilogue

Ellen McCallie had twelve children, but only six lived to adulthood. Despite her large family, Ellen participated in many community activities. She opened her home to traveling ministers and anyone in need, requiring her children to treat even unwelcome visitors with kindness. Two of her sons started McCallie School for boys in Chattanooga. Her daughter, Grace McCallie, co-founded the Girls' Preparatory School.

Chapter Eight

Foreign Country

Emilie Todd Helm, half sister to Mary Lincoln
September 23, 1863
Atlanta, Georgia
A native of Kentucky, Emilie found herself a widow without a home after she accompanied her husband to the Confederacy. Her husband, Ben Helm, fought to establish the Confederacy Could she get back to Kentucky and accept her husband's death?

* * *

Emilie glanced at her watch again, and her shoulder muscles knotted even tighter. Couldn't the carriage driver go faster? She couldn't be late. If only she hadn't left Atlanta. Her choice forced someone else to care for Ben, and she hated the outcome.

Looking back, she wished Ben had accepted Lincoln's job offer and stayed with the Union—he'd be alive today. Her sister, Mary Lincoln, would have loved to have them in Washington. Ben refused because he longed to help the newly-formed Confederacy.

Her sister, Elodie, leaned so close that her brown curls brushed Emilie's cheek. "Stop fretting. Your watch is always fast because it needs cleaning. We'll arrive on time."

Emilie gazed off into the distance. Caring for watches seemed useless in light of her sorrow. If only she could get to the church. Perhaps then she could make arrangements—rather than weep. Her husband believed this war boiled down to states' rights and feared the Federal government might crush out freedom. She and Ben agreed to support the Confederacy together, even thought it meant leaving their Kentucky home. He raised troops from among his friends and offered them to the newly-formed nation. The Confederacy allowed him to command his Kentucky brigade, at least at first. While Ben fought she didn't mind moving from place to place to stay close by. Not now.

Go home. Why had the maid made her corset so snug? She couldn't draw air. Would life ever return to normal? Her arms ached for an embrace from her husband. Widow! Such a nasty word. Her head throbbed. How could she make a living and clothe the children? Would she ever gain control of her life again? Why would God allow this? After all, Ben was better than most men. He didn't get drunk and chase other women. She swallowed back the sobs that caught in her throat. No one must think her weak. The service started at eleven, but Emilie refused to prod the driver again. Rudeness and impatience never helped. A Southern lady considered those around her, and so she must.

Distract yourself.

Atlanta. People ambled alongside the road smiling. Several ladies occupied rocking chairs on a front porch to her left, as if they had nothing urgent. One woman frowned and shielded her eyes as the horses galloped past. Was she trying to see who hurried so? Or was she shading her eyes? The sun seared Emilie's. How dare it blaze with such fury. Instead the clouds should weep for her.

If only we get there in time. At last the carriage slowed at an Episcopal church. She attended a Scottish Presbyterian, but as long as the minister preached the Gospel, she didn't mind. Men in gray uniforms swarmed about the entrance. Her stomach whirled. There it was—the hearse. Her husband's body lay inside. Benjamin Hardin Helm was dead. Now she couldn't pretend he might come home. A shudder ran along her spine as soldiers lifted the coffin onto their shoulders.

A pine box? Surely something more elegant could be acquired for a general.

"There she is."

"It's his wife."

General Breckenridge whipped off his hat as he approached the carriage. He smoothed his dark hair before opening the door and offering his hand to Emile. "Mrs. Helm, I am quite pleased you could make it."

Emilie took his hand and stepped onto the road. Light reflected off medals on his chest as she gazed into his dark eyes. This wasn't a good time, but she must voice her request. Winsome manners. Her mother taught her that, and she managed to get things done without upsetting anyone—a true Southern belle. The Confederacy might not consider Kentucky part of the South. Nevertheless, Emilie clung to her southern heritage. "Ben would prefer to rest in Kentucky." Tears escaped, and she released his hand to grab a handkerchief. "Is … there any way we can send his body home?"

Breckenridge wrinkled his brow and tugged at his long mustache. "I am sorry, madam. How I wish we could. I thought the world of your husband. But in time of war—"

"I understand." She stepped backward only to bump into Eloise who now stood behind her. She must exude grace and hope for the best. "I thought since he was a general…"

"Yes, we try to accommodate widows of our commanding officers." He cleared his throat. "But the difficulties of transferring a body back …"

She offered a weak smile, though tears continued to flow against her will. "Please inquire about that, please. It would mean so much."

"Yes, ma'am." Breckinridge offered his arm. "May I escort you inside the church? We are about to start the service."

"Thank you." She took his arm and followed behind the casket. Unbelievable. Only a few weeks before, Ben left for Chickamauga, Georgia. Her lips burned as she recalled the touch of his last kiss and the light in his blue eyes. If only she could turn back the clock. But would she tell Ben not to follow orders? If she'd stayed here with the Dabney family, General Bragg would have found her after Ben was shot. Ben might have lived had she cared for him. At the very least she would have planned his funeral. Pain radiated to her throat at the thought.

Why would God allow this tragedy?

Breckenridge seated her on the first row, and Eloide sat beside her. Emilie cringed at the opened coffin before her. Surely they embalmed him, or the warm weather would force them to bury him right away. Horrible thought.

Ben's face was so pale and rigid, nothing like the loving warmth she experienced weeks ago. How much pain did he endure with an abdominal wound? She gritted her teeth. If only she could die. How could she raise a son and two daughters without him? The congregation sang *Amazing Grace* and she moved her lips to the words. She could sing it from memory, but today nothing came from her clogged throat. Next came *Rock of Ages*. If only the familiar words could soothe her soul. Tears kept coming, sometimes dripping when she failed to catch them. The song faded and the minister opened his Bible. "The Lord giveth and the Lord taketh away. Blessed be the name of the Lord."

"Amen."

"Amen."

Emilie's lips quivered. Right now she did not want to bless anyone. The God she worshiped possessed the power to prevent her grief. Didn't he love her? If so, why didn't he spare her this horror? The world was empty and cold, and her future bleak. If only she could be home, somewhere safe—where she made the choices. She must stiffen herself and endure.

"It is appointed unto men once to die, and after that the judgment." The minister lifted his hand. "Death will visit us all. Are you prepared to face God? You can't stand before him with your sins unforgiven, but Jesus paid the price so we can have peace with God."

I can't listen. I know what comes next.

"In John three it says, '"He that believeth on the Son hath everlasting life: and he that believeth not the Son shall not see life; but the wrath of God abideth on him.' General Helm believed, so we know his destiny."

Did he? She took a deep breath to stave off the nausea. Emilie explained her faith so many times. Ben didn't mind, and he encouraged her to attend services. He respected Christianity, but he thought he could please God without assistance. Did he trust Christ in those terrible moments prior to death? A gag convulsed her throat.

No. He can't be in hell!

Right now she'd love to scold him for causing so much pain. Why couldn't he accept the forgiveness Jesus offered? Stubborn man. His choice meant she'd never see him again.

Oh, dear! Now she lashed out at her husband's memory. How could she stoop so low? God must judge, not men. Her husband had faced God already. Who was she to pass sentence?

Mrs. Todd sat beside her daughter and pulled several sheets of paper from her handbag. "See? Governor John Helm petitioned Lincoln for you."

"So Ben's father had to ask. It took a governor to rescue me." She massaged her temples. The Confederates let her down after her husband gave his life for their cause. "I requested a pass from General Bragg right after … the funeral. But I heard nothing from him."

"Perhaps something went wrong with the message."

"Bragg sent a telegram to General Grant. I should think he had the authority. I've been so uneasy because I feel in the way. Mrs. Dabney wanted me to remain with her, but she barely accommodated her own family."

"Do you have enough money to travel?"

"I hope so. I received my husband's pay, a mere pittance." Emilie sighed. "Ben grows apace, so I bought him clothes. The girls have frocks from both the Bruce and Dabney families."

"How are they?"

"Ben does not recall his father." The words stung. Her son would never know his father's sterling character. Her chest was heavy with that thought. "The girls cried, but they became accustomed to his long absences. Now they speak of him sometimes. I usually cry, but . . . "

"You're in mourning, Emilie. That's expected." Mrs. Todd took her hand. "Think about going home. I have railroad maps. We must plot our course back."

Emilie inhaled and bit her lip. Surely she saved enough money.

* * *

Emilie's fingers went numb. Seventeen-month-old Ben slept in her right arm. She shifted her sleeping baby and managed not to wake him. He fussed several hours earlier in the day. What a dreadful sound inside a train, or in this case, a steamer. She sacrificed comfort to get the cheapest seats.

"Shall I take him for you?" Her mother held out her arms. She sat across the aisle with four-year-old Elodie, who was named after Emilie's sister. Six-year-old Katherine leaned against Emilie's arm, napping. For days they rode in train cars or waited in depots. If only they could arrive soon. "Hmm. How much longer?"

Her mother leaned toward the window, narrowing her eyes. "We're nearing Fort Monroe now."

"I shall let him sleep." She rubbed his back, hoping he didn't cry when she had to get up.

"Let me hold him while you show your pass."

Emilie nodded.

A uniformed officer marched in with a speaking trumpet and turned to face the travelers. "May I have your attention, please? I am an officer of the United States Navy. Each of you must take an oath of allegiance before landing. We'll talk to you one-by-one."

Heat rushed to Emilie's face. "What did he say?"

Mrs. Todd shook her head. "Don't worry. Show your document from Lincoln."

"I hope so. We came here under a flag of truce, and that ought to tell them I mean no harm."

Moments later she stood in a small cabin. The Navy Lieutenant sat behind a desk and held out a quill. "Mrs. Helm, all I need is your signature on this oath of allegiance to the Union. After that you may go ashore."

Unthinkable. She glared at him, her face blazing. Her mother's words echoed in her mind. Winsome manners worked. People respond to kindness. But an image of her husband's cold body appeared. Her stomach cramped. They murdered him. Could she be polite at such a time? Could anyone? "Signature?"

"Yes. That's all we need." He smiled and pointed to the paper.

"Sign your name here."

"No."

"Excuse me?" His smile vanished.

"I…cannot do that."

He scratched his temple. "Why?"

"You killed my husband." Her voice quivered, but it was hard to say these words.

His mouth fell open. "Ma'am?"

"The Union army took my husband's life. I won't and can't sign that paper because I can't promise allegiance to the country that killed him."

"I am sorry about your husband, ma'am—"

"His name was General Helm, Lieutenant."

"What's the problem?" A Lieutenant Commander stepped in the door.

Emilie put a gloved hand over her eyes. Ben often warned her about her temper. Her fiery words didn't meet her standards for polite conversation. Now what would she do? Would they let her go home anyway?

The Lieutenant licked his lips. "Mrs. Helm does not wish to swear allegiance."

"Ma'am, we cannot allow you to leave this ship unless you do," the lieutenant commander snatched her papers. "Do you wish to return to the Confederacy?"

She pictured the solemnities at her husband's grave. Such horrors should happen much later in life. "No."

"These say you live in Kentucky. Are you traveling there?" The commander spoke in soft tones.

"Yes." She trembled as she considered her options, which were few.

"I can help you get there, if you sign this." He held up the oath.

She swallowed. They had no idea of her pain, but she could

never sign. Ever. "No."

"We shall consult with the admiral."

Tears poured down her face.

An hour later, the Lieutenant Commander returned with a sheaf of papers. "Mrs. Helm, we shall send you to the White House."

She gasped. What had she done? She never intended to involve her sister. Had she misunderstood? "I live in Kentucky."

He held up a telegram. "The president ordered it."

Her neck and shoulders grew damp with perspiration.

I want to go home.

* * *

The White House

November 1863

Emilie gave the huge entrance hall and white columns a mere glance before she collapsed into her sister's arms and wept. Memories of Abe with Ben flashed into her mind, and her loss stung more than ever. At least here her family might understand her grief. What a blessed relief to release the pain with those who cared. But she still must use some restraint since Katherine came with her.

Mary cried too, with deep wrenching sobs, which echoed in the hallway.

Did she love Ben that much? Emilie released Mary and gazed at her older sister. Mary's blue eyes were bloodshot and her face blotchy red, as if she'd cried much longer. Where was Mary's sunny disposition? "Sister, how are you?"

Mary hiccuped and sniffled, as she touched a wadded handkerchief to her nose. "I'm broken hearted about your husband. Abe thought so much of him. We have our own sorrows, too. Did you hear we lost Willie?"

"No! What happened?"

Mary shook her head. "A fever. The doctors couldn't devise a

"Most of the time I kept to my room, but the general arrived while I sat with Mary." Emilie's cheeks got hot. She hated to think she violated her own values. In this case, the man provoked her. "The General made embarrassing remarks about the victory at Chattanooga and made me angry. I should have held my tongue."

"I told him the Todd family used words like darts." His wide lips curled into a momentary smile. "Of course, he doesn't have my familial affection for you, so he took exception to my remark."

Now Emilie's cheeks blazed. How often did she fall short of her own standards? If she believed Abe, she failed more than she realized. Since her husband died she spoke with more sharpness, but Abe's words indicated a lifetime habit.

He winked. "And now I wonder if I have upset you, little sister."

She shrugged. "I'd prefer to excuse myself as a broken-hearted widow, but I suppose I can't."

"This war impacts us all, Emilie." The skin on his face sagged. "Yesterday I overheard our children arguing. When I went to referee, I learned your Katherine insisted Jefferson Davis filled the office of president. My son maintained that I was president. It made me quite sad that the cousins could not get along, but their spat exemplifies what we face. I am truly sorry."

Tears moistened Emilie's eyes. Such separation between loved ones should never occur. If only she could have gone straight to Kentucky rather than stopping here. "I need to go home."

"Ah, but you will not find peace there." He raised one lanky hand. "Both Union and Confederate sympathizers live there. Your husband's choice might cause trouble for you."

"At least I shall not be here making politics more difficult."

He raised an eyebrow. "If you are determined, then I shall write a letter for you. As long as you don't break any laws, I can protect you from Union harassment."

His face aged a lot since the war started. If only she could turn back the clock to the times that she and Ben visited the Lincolns. Sweet memory! "Thank you, Abe. I shall not do anything to make you ashamed. I promise."

"I know, Emilie. I trust you."

It was time to go, and she inched toward the door.

* * *

Summer 1864

What on earth? Emilie's heart took off at a clip as she gazed out her kitchen window where Union soldiers marched into her garden and partook the fresh vegetables she grew. Still holding her son, she yanked herself away from her youngest daughter's grasp and stomped outside. The Lieutenant directing the men frowned and waved her away.

Growing hotter by the minute, she ignored his directions and barreled up to him.

"Sir, what do you think you are doing on my property?"

"What makes you dislike Union soldiers, madam?" The man spread his legs and put both hands on his waist.

Ben squirmed as if he wanted to get down, but she shifted him so she had a better grip. What a terrible predicament. She must avoid talking about her husband's role in the war. The last thing she wanted was a fight in front of her children. "You have no right to steal my food, sir. Please leave."

"You don't like us because your husband fought for the South." The man came nearer. "Isn't that your problem? Mrs. Helm?"

"Get off my property." She tried to look fierce, but how scary could a woman be holding a toddler? One soldier grabbed several chickens and headed for the road. So much for coming home. How did Lincoln know she might encounter trouble? What did he hear?

"Put those chickens back where they belong, young man." She

put down her son to pluck the animals free while Ben pulled at the grass around him. Holding two squawking hens, she scurried back to the Lieutenant. "What makes you think you can get by with breaking the law?"

The man placed a hand on his gun. "You have no authority to make me leave."

"I have a letter from President Lincoln." She pointed back toward her house. "You don't want to tangle with him."

"Oh!" The soldier chuckled. "The rebel lady looks angry. What should we do?"

Another soldier rode up on a horse. "Excuse me, sir. General Burbridge needs your men for maneuvers."

"I shall bring him my letter and file a formal complaint."

The men hurried off.

Emilie sighed and whispered a prayer of thanks.

Eloide stood in the door. "Mama, I'm hungry. Can we eat now?"

"Yes." Emilie glanced over her shoulder at the retreating men. "I shall ensure those men won't bother us."

She sat the children down to eat. "Dear Jesus, I thank you for this food and for my family. We know all we have comes from you, and we beg for your provision. In Jesus name I pray, amen."

And Lord, I can't talk in front of the children. But I'm desperate. Help me find a way to keep food on the table. On several occasions the Confederacy had paid her husband in cotton, but the bales always seemed to get destroyed before she could fetch them. Her money dwindled, and she must find income.

Once the children ate, she allowed them to play around her feet so she could sip her coffee. She flipped open the paper to the want ads. Her gaze landed on an ad for a church organist in Cincinnati.

If only that job was here in Kentucky.

She massaged her forehead. Last night several soldiers carried off a pie she left in the window to cool. The week before, men slipped inside and took her freshly baked bread while she changed a diaper. Plus, staunch Union men harassed her when she shopped. Perhaps she should relocate. In Ohio her husband's name would not create a problem. She had friends there. Emilie mastered the organ at a Cincinnati conservatory before she married. Such a job would allow her to stay home with the children. Maybe a move would be the best thing, especially since she dreaded even leaving the house.

Later in the day, while the children slept, she penned a letter to ask about the job. *Lord, help me to find a home.*

* * *

1884

Helm Family Cemetery, Lexington Kentucky

Emilie stood beside the fresh grave. The familiar twinge in her stomach reminded her of the sorrow she endured. So much had happened. But her time was running out, and she had several things to say. "Ben, it's been twenty-one years, and I still miss you. I accepted God's sovereignty even though I don't understand your early death. He guided me to jobs. At first I served as an organist, and now I work for the postal service here in Kentucky. I hope you accepted Jesus because I want to see you in heaven."

A racket behind her turned out to be her daughter's carriage driving up.

"Ugh." Katherine hopped out and hurried to Emilie, throwing an arm around her mother's shoulders. "Surely they'll bring something to cover the dirt. The sight of that ugly black soil would make anybody cry."

"I'm fine, dear. Besides I think they plan on a spray of flowers." Emilie smiled at her grown daughter. "It's wonderful to have him home where he belongs."

Katherine shook her head. "I wish I recalled more. Daddy's

those thoughts. Sorrows tore at her heart, and she didn't have confidence that God existed anymore. "Is there life after death, Papa? I'm desperate for answers."

Her eyes brimmed with tears.

A soft tread sounded behind her.

"Mama," Frittie said.

"Frittie! Why are you awake?" Her stomach lurched. She scooped him up, handling him with a gentle grip. The lightest touch on his skin left a nasty bruise.

He needed special care, and nursing came natural to her. Even as a child, she looked after her younger siblings. Now she sponsored a hospital in her district and often corresponded with Florence Nightingale.

Frittie sank his face into Alice's plush robe.

"You must go back to bed," Alice whispered into his soft, brown hair. She caressed his pale skin. Would lack of sleep endanger his health?

Frittie touched her face. "Mama, are you crying?"

"Yes." Alice whispered. "Sometimes I think about my father, and I miss him. You will miss your daddy when he goes off with the soldiers, too."

"Will they fight?" Frittie asked.

"No." Alice rubbed her son's back. "Papa won't have to give orders, so he will come home soon."

"Good!" Frittie's face lit up.

If only she could be reassured so easily. The sorrows she endured weighed on her heart. Frittie's fragile health kept her so tense. The doctors expected him to die young. Would that be best for him? He hated the agony. She shouldn't allow that thought to surface. What mother would want that?

"Let's go back to bed," Alice ascended the stairs and tucked her son under the covers. She remained outside his door until she heard his regular breathing, and then headed down the steps again to the kitchen. At the rustic sink, she filled the teakettle and sat down to wait.

If only she could discuss the ideas Strauss taught, she could find the answer.

The kettle whistled. Alice prepared tea and added milk and sugar. She sipped and savored its warmth and delicate flavor, hoping her muscles would relax again.

Papa advised her to pray for guidance. She buried her head in her hands. But how could she pray with doubts? She'd nursed too many dying patients. First grandmother died, then Papa, and then so many soldiers passed from injuries in the wars. Is Frittie next? God, do you exist? Where are you?

After she finished, she ran water into the sink and washed dishes. Papa never left a mess for the cook, and his influence lived—even if he did not.

* * *

The following morning, May 29

As the sun peeked through the windows, Frittie sat up. Sounds came from his father's room, and Frittie longed to see him. His father always left with all his medals and his sword. "Ernst, I hear Papa. Wake up!"

Frittie threw off the blue-and-white quilted bedspread and slid from his child-sized brass bed onto the patchwork rug. He scampered into the hallway to the banisters at the top of the stairs. In the foyer below, Father consulted with a manservant. Bright sunshine sparkled on the enormous sword at his side. Frittie's small body stiffened to give a parting salute—like his father did.

I want my Papa.

With a sigh, he turned on his heel and marched back to his room. Frittie rummaged in his toy box to find a toy sword. "Let's play war!"

"No!" Alice screamed. This cannot be happening. She grabbed her robe as she ran from the room.

Still wearing a gown, Victoria appeared in her doorway, eyes widened. "What happened?"

"Your brother fell." Alice pushed past her and hurried down the steps donning her robe as she ran. The windows. Why didn't she think about the children before we opened them all? This is my fault. He fell several stories. Was he alive? She had to get there fast.

A handful of servants stood about his body on the patio. "I think he's breathing."

The cook shook her head. "He's not going to survive this one."

"I doubt there's hope." The housekeeper's frown deepened. "He looks terrible. The poor child almost died of the flu."

Fire streaked up Alice's spine as she knelt. Frittie's face looked ashen and his breathing rasped shallow. She rubbed his clammy hands. No broken bones, no visible bleeding, but he could be bleeding inside.

"What will the prince do?" A housemaid moved closer. "He'll never make it home before…"

"Please, stop." Alice's throat constricted. She glanced up, and the maid froze. "I see no external injuries. Frittie! Frittie. Can you hear me?"

"It's no use."

"Who said that?" She looked around, but no one met her gaze. "Get me some smelling salts.

Ernst shoved them toward her.

Alice waved the smelling salts under his nose. This had to work. She could not lose her son. "Frittie, talk to me, honey."

He did not respond.

Her chest grew tighter, and she had to force air into her lungs. Could this be a dream? Ever since they discovered his hemophilia, fear for him haunted her ... *I'm not just a mother. I am a nurse. Why can't I think? God, if you really exist, please assist me.*

Alice looked about the crowd again, and spotted the butler. "Herr Schneider?"

He stepped forward.

"Please contact his doctor." She turned to the housekeeper. "And get me a basin of warm water and towels. Frederick, please carry him to his bed—carefully."

Alice ran behind the footman and peered over his shoulder. With an injury of that nature, the head and spine must be kept aligned, something she feared attempting. Frederick did well, except he tread on every squeaky stair, and the squeal made her grind her teeth. But then, her muscles and nerves were rigid. She witnessed death before and knew its forboding presence.

The housekeeper met them in Frittie's bedroom. She already arranged the room so the doctor had easy access to Frittie's bed. Water and sponges stood ready. Herr Schneider arrived with writing paper for her notes and a chair from the library.

Once in bed, Frittie's chalky face constricted Alice's throat. A bruise grew on his forehead. Pushing aside dark thoughts, she sponged his face and hands while calling his name, but to no avail.

Forty-five minutes later, Doctor Eigenbrodt arrived. A tall man with a ruddy complexion, he bowed and offered a smile. A shorter man stood beside him. Both men carried black bags. "Your Majesty, I brought a colleague, Doctor Schmidt."

She offered her hand and a weak smile. "Thank you for coming, sirs."

"I understand your son had an accident," Doctor Eigenbrodt said.

If only she'd kept those windows closed, but the doctor asked for facts. Guilt would not heal her son. "He fell from a window."

"How far did he fall?"

As soon as she said the words, the doctor would lose interest. Medicine held few treatments for a free bleeder. Her hands longed for some action, some treatment to hold back death. "He fell two stories and landed on pavement."

Doctor Eigenbrodt pressed his lips together. "The prince suffers from hemophilia."

His colleague nodded. "I see."

Both men moved toward the bed. Eigenbrodt pulled out a reflex hammer and stethoscope.

Alice stepped away, but kept her gaze trained on the two men. Working at the hospital during two Hessian wars, she learned medical language and procedures.

Doctor Schmidt spoke in a low voice. "He does not react to deep pain."

"Yes." Doctor Eigenbrodt pinched his nose. "None of the normal reflexes appear."

Alice placed a hand on her throat. Those technical words meant her son's prognosis was poor. The room grew darker.

Doctor Eigenbrodt spoke in a husky voice. "You can be sure there's internal bleeding. There is no way to stop it and the pressure on his brain."

Doctor Schmidt shrugged. "Ja, and the pressure …"

Eigenbrodt looked at her and shook his head. "I am sorry, Madam."

The room reeled, but Alice took several deep breaths. She recalled her mother all those years ago. She refused to believe Papa was dying until the end. Should she follow Mama's example and pretend there was hope? Wasn't there always a tiny ray? She would do what she could. If only she had her parent's faith.

"Has Doctor Luft found any useful preparations?" Doctor Eigenbrodt spoke to his colleague.

"None. We could try Adler, but—Dr Schmidt lifted his palms

and shook his head.

Alice clapped a shaky hand over her mouth. Somehow she must stay in control.

Doctor Eigenbrodt addressed Herr Schneider. "I'm afraid you must contact the Crown Prince immediately."

"We have sent a messenger," Schneider said with a nod.

Alice strained to catch further discussion as the men moved out of the room. Nothing. They would explain matters to her husband, but they avoided her gaze. Doubtless they did not like her willingness to work alongside them. She learned so much from Florence Nightingale, who expanded the role of nurses

Alice walked back to the bed and caressed her son's forehead. He was such a lovely, sweet child. Why must he face death? She grabbed a pencil and started keeping records—anything to keep the dark thoughts at bay. Every fifteen minutes she recorded Frittie's pulse and respirations. And she bathed his face, crooning lullabies. Tears stung her eyes as she noted his uneven breathing and clammy skin.

Please, do not leave me.

The sun sank below the horizon, and Frittie took a final deep breath. His body went limp.

Alice crumpled onto his chest releasing her sobs.

A hand touched her shoulder, and she glanced up.

Tears coursed down her husband's face and mingled with his dark beard. "Come. They must prepare the body."

She stood, but swayed.

Louis scooped her up and carried her to bed. "Your health is fragile too. Get some rest."

She pulled herself to a sitting position, but nothing seemed real. I must make … plans. Somehow.

* * *

Alice picked up a glove and pulled it on, working her fingers as

apostle Peter said, 'We have not followed cunningly devised fables when we made known unto you the power and coming of our Lord Jesus Christ, but we were eyewitnesses of his majesty.'"

"I should wish to believe that, sir."

"You can believe it. Peter recorded his testimony in the Bible, the Word of God. Despite the threat of a martyr's death, the apostle did not alter his testimony."

Baum frowned. "Peter suffered a martyr's death? I daresay he would not give his life for a lie."

"I daresay none." Baum shook his head as he spoke.

Feeling like an intruder, Alice motioned for Christa Schenck. Both moved toward the nurses' desk at the end of the room while the two men talked. After a few moments, Robertson knelt by the bed, and the patient's haggard face relaxed. When the minister concluded his prayer, he and the soldier talked in muted tones. Baum smiled when the minister rose to leave.

On the ride home, the clergyman chatted with Christa Schenck about the fine horses that pulled the carriage. Alice settled back on the cushions and said nothing. She did her duty, but depleted her strength. As the carriage swayed back and forth, she mulled over the clergyman's instructions to Baum.

We did not follow cunningly devised fables.

* * *

A week later, the guests were gone, and home life returned to a predictable routine. Each morning as she woke, Alice listened for Frittie's footsteps. Then with a pang, she'd remember. She missed his warm kisses and gifts of wildflowers. Her thoughts returned often to the family tomb, where his body rested.

One evening, after her lady-in-waiting retired, Alice sat down in her office to find comfort. She picked up a letter from Strauss.

The Journey

Dearest Princess Alice,

I offer my deepest condolences to you and your dear husband. The pain must be wretched. However, your son suffers no more. He does not demand your tenderness and care. Enshrine his memory in your heart. Now that he has departed, draw your remaining children into your embrace. Please accept my heartfelt sympathy.

Sincerely,

David F. Strauss

Alice flung the letter across the room. Empty words. She wanted her son, not some memory enshrined in her heart.

She burst into tears and sobbed till her body was limp.

Strauss used his usual arrogant tone, but he hadn't spoken of God. Without all-powerful God, no one can have compassion.

Alice took a deep breath and placed a hand on her throat. She must think through the issues and come to some conclusion. Papa said Scripture was logical and would prove itself. Strauss taught that miracles are contrary to nature and therefore illogical. He said Jesus did not perform miracles. Instead, his followers exaggerated stories about him and created myths.

She sighed and rubbed her hands over her face. The two men contradicted. Papa believed a miracle is beyond our understanding, but not irrational. An all-powerful God would control nature.

Her body seared with heat, and she smacked the desk. "I cannot resolve this! Frittie, I miss you. The ache is too intense. I cannot think! Oh God, I must have help! If you are there, please help me. Do you exist?"

A memory popped into her mind. "Reverend Robertson mentioned eyewitnesses. I remember reading about witnesses who saw Jesus after the resurrection."

Alice pushed back the chair and walked to the bookcase opposite her desk. Her Bible, buried under several books, sat on the bottom shelf. She brushed away dust and returned to the desk where she searched the once-familiar pages until she turned to 1st Corinthians.

I found it! The fifteenth chapter. Papa spoke of this "…he rose again the third day according to the Scriptures, and that he was seen of Cephas, then of the twelve. After that he was seen of above five hundred brethren at once, of whom the greater part remain until this present."

The passage did not sound like myth. The writer spoke of five hundred living witnesses who saw Jesus after his death. Courts settled cases with one or two witnesses. Evidence pointed to Jesus's resurrection. Tears slid down her cheeks. The philosophical framework she built with Strauss crumbled.

Memories flooded her mind of Papa preparing her for confirmation. He brushed aside politicians to spend hours with her. One night he explained the sign of the resurrection.

"Religious leaders asked Jesus for a sign to prove his teachings. Jesus told them he would 'destroy this temple and in three days I will raise it up.'" The resurrection fulfilled the sign."

Alice bit her lip. Strauss believed that resurrection was a miracle and not logical. But God would grant grace and comfort. Strauss' words meant something else—a spiritual meaning, robbing the world of hope.

She spoke aloud, "I want hope!" Warmth flooded her heart as she realized Papa and Frittie still exist. They are together in heaven. *Almighty Father, forgive me. I should have asked for your guidance earlier.*

She clasped her hands together and took a slow, deep breath. Papa died before Frittie's birth. But she pictured her father twirling her son about at their first meeting. What a heavenly image. A sigh escaped Alice's lips as she smiled.

From the drawer she retrieved a stack of sympathy letters from her mother. Deep concern had prompted her to write almost every day. Alice thumbed through them. Despite their black borders, Mama spoke of her father and eternal life.

Thank you for trying to bring me back, Mama.

Alice stood straighter and taller. Frittie loved music, so she had not played the piano since he died. As she walked toward the piano in the drawing room, she searched her memory for the piano composition her father wrote for Psalm 100. Today she wanted to play it again.

"Precious Savior, please tell Papa I came back. It was a tedious journey, but I am safe now. He will want to know."

Alice played.

Make a joyful noise unto the Lord, all ye lands.
Serve the Lord with gladness,
Come before his presence with singing.
Know ye that the Lord, he is God.
It is he that hath made us and not we ourselves.
We are his people and the sheep of his pasture.
Enter into his gates with thanksgiving
and into his courts with praise.
Be thankful unto him, and bless his name.
For the Lord is good; and his mercy is everlasting,
And his truth endureth to all generations.
(KJV)

Epilogue

Alice enjoyed a warm relationship with her father and longed for him the rest of her life. She loved deep discussions with him, and soon realized her husband didn't have the ability to discuss weighty

stumbled across the room to open the red damask curtains. The afternoon sun streamed into the apartment, bouncing off the mirror over her fireplace, crystal whatnots on the mantel, and the silver frame that held her mother's photo.

For a moment she basked in the warmth. The contract bound her to silence in life, but not in death. She scurried to her French provincial desk where she located paper and ink. She held her pen aloft and puckered her brows.

* * *

1828

I want the prince. Caroline did a double pirouette in her full-length mirror, bowed, and launched into her dance from the previous night. Her whole body tingled as she poured energy into the dance. She flung her arms wide, but her hand struck a table lamp that teetered and crashed to the floor.

Mother tended to fuss about her impulsive ways.

"Caroline? What happened?" Mrs. Bauer, her mother, entered frowning.

"Sorry." She dropped several large pieces in the dustbin. "I was dancing before the prince again. And I saw him smile at me."

Mrs. Bauer's thin lips flattened as she stooped to pick up the glass. "Be careful, dear. You forget yourself. Between broken glass and spilled oil, you must not dance until I clean."

Caroline dropped onto her brass bed as her heart floated away. "It was Prince Leopold from your home—Coburg, Germany. His story is so romantic. Even though his wife died eleven years ago, he still grieves for her. How odd that he would come to my performance."

Her mother, who held a fragment of glass, turned to gaze at Caroline. "You are sure? It was really Prince Leopold?"

"I saw him, Mama. What a dream. He had dark hair and was so handsome." She sat up and put her feet on the hand-crocheted

rug by her bed. "Mama, you must introduce us while he's in town."

Her mother knelt to mop up the oil. "I have not had contact with him for years. Remember, dear, I was just a playmate — not an aristocrat."

"Tell me about him."

Her mother put down the dustbin. "We are about the same age. He and I played together as children. Even as a child, he was handsome, with all his dark hair and noble face. He fell in love with Charlotte. She was the only child of George the Fourth and heir to the British throne."

"And she died in childbirth."

"Yes." Mrs. Bauer nodded while sweeping up the last of the glass. "My nephew, Christian Stockmar, works as Prince Leopold's secretary."

"And the prince never recovered?" Caroline imagined the man swooning over her beauty.

"That is the rumor."

Caroline went to the large wardrobe opposite her bed and pulled out the glittery red costume she'd worn the night before. Holding it up to her body, she posed in the mirror. "I cheered him up last night. I saw him smile."

Dustbin in one hand, the broom and rag in the other, Mrs. Bauer paused in the doorway. "You could see him while you danced?"

"Yes. He was in the huge box to my left. He looks just like they described him—dark and melancholy."

A knock sounded on the door.

"I'll get it." She tossed her outfit on the bed and danced out of her room, through the small apartment to the door. She opened it to a man wearing a dark green uniform.

"My name is Huhnlein," the chubby man said. "Prince Leopold wishes to visit Miss Caroline Bauer."

"I am Caroline Bauer. Please tell the prince to come up." Then she turned to her mother, who followed her to the door. "Mama, it's the prince."

"This is quite an honor." Her mother smiled and fluffed Caroline's blonde curls.

"Prince Leopold," the servant announced with a solemn bow. In a moment, Prince Leopold stood at the door. Holding his tall frame erect, he strode into the tiny room. He had a small mouth, long oval face, prominent nose, and large, chestnut-colored eyes. Towering over the ladies, he wore a knee-length wool coat buttoned up to his chin against the December wind.

A chill went up Caroline's spine as she bowed.

"Caroline Bauer?" he said, holding his monocle to one eye.

"Yes, Your Majesty," Caroline said.

"Your performance last night was superb."

"Thank you, sir." Caroline trained her eyes on the floor rather than his face. "I am honored."

"I believe you are my former playmate," He turned to Mrs. Bauer. "You look well. Stockmar sends you greetings."

"Thank you." She lowered her head. "I hope Christian is well?"

"Indeed, Ma'am." He chuckled. "Of course, he worries about his stomach, but I daresay that's his medical training."

"Yes. How well I recall his hypochondria." She nodded. "His stomach annoys him when he's worried."

"I had hoped to speak with your daughter alone, so if you will excuse us for a moment." His brown eyes bored into Caroline, and he dismissed Mrs. Bauer with a wave of his hand.

"Of course, Your Majesty. I shall wait in the next room."

"Your Majesty, please sit here," Caroline pointed to their austere sofa and hoped he did not notice how worn it looked.

He sat and motioned for her to join him. "Come, please, sit here

beside me."

She perched on the opposite end of the couch and stared at her clenched hands. Her face burned like fire. At last she looked up and met his gaze.

"Sir? Do … I displease you?"

"On the contrary, I find you ravishing." His gaze held hers. "Are you in love with anyone?"

"Not at all." A tremor ran up her back. "Opportunities arose …"

"Yes?" A deep line furrowed his brow.

"But, I … refused them all," she said. She squeezed her hands until the knuckles turned white.

"Could you love me?" he inched closer to her. His dark wig looked stiff, and she detected creases around his mouth. "You have stirred my heart."

"Uh, well …" she murmured, trying to scoot away. She twisted the edge of her sleeve.

"Despite all my titles and privileges, I am weary. I have searched for a lady to devote herself to me—as my wife. Could you go away with me and live secluded forever?"

She felt his breath on her neck, and her skin tingled. Is this what she wanted? Would she sell herself for money?

"I will keep you safe and love you, sweet lady. If you marry me, I can give enough income to make you comfortable."

A prince wants to marry her? Expenses stretched Caroline's meager salary to the limit. Her brother had asked for another loan, but costumes were expensive. A pile of bills awaited her even now. She focused on his eyes again and her heart quivered. "I can— try to love you." Caroline blushed and looked away.

"Ah, you are so lovely." His massive arms crushed her in a long embrace.

Trembling from head to toe, she remained stiff in his arms.

Her mother crossed the creaky floor to open the door.

"Christian, come in." Mrs. Bauer waved her nephew into the tiny room. "We expected the prince."

Caroline collapsed on the bed. "A-a-h!"

"You thought the prince would come here?" Christian raised one eyebrow. "No, he would not be seen here."

"Then why did you ask us to come to this dreadful place?" Caroline sat up and crossed her arms.

Mrs. Bauer offered her nephew a straight chair. "Yes, please explain."

Stockmar eased himself into the chair. "The Prince must be cautious. His mother would forbid this marriage, should she hear of it."

"His mother, the Dowager Duchess?" Mrs. Bauer's eyes grew wide.

"Yes, you must not underestimate the power of his mother. She is a clever lady," Stockmar raised a finger. "And the Prince could lose his income."

Caroline's mouth fell open. That would not work. "What? Lose his money?"

"He received a salary for life when he married the princess. However, the English might take exception to another marriage. They could discontinue his salary," Stockmar said.

"Then why does he pursue such a plan?" Mrs. Bauer said.

Caroline nodded. For once she agreed with her mother.

"The prince suffered terribly after his wife's death."

Caroline touched her cheek. "My face helped him to put aside his grief."

Stockmar pursed his lips. "Leopold now longs for companionship, and I must keep him from a lady of the night. He is prepared to endow a large sum on Caroline when they marry, but she must agree to secrecy."

Mrs. Bauer spoke, "He's attracted to the wrong kind of lady? I can assure you my daughter—"

"But Mama." One way or the other, she would marry that man. Her mother must be jealous because she didn't get a prince. "Be careful what you say."

"No, Cousin." Stockmar held up a finger. "Let me warn you, he is attempting to acquire the Greek throne. If he does, his offer ends."

Mrs. Bauer's face reddened. "He's trying to become King of Greece?"

"No." Caroline huffed, rubbing a hand over her face. "That's not good."

Stockmar shrugged. "It is unlikely he will succeed."

"Thank goodness. When can I see him?" Caroline clasped her hands together.

"Tomorrow, I will take you to see Prince Leopold."

"Ah, yes!" Caroline squealed with delight and twirled herself about.

"Christian, we need your wise counsel." Mrs. Bauer touched his hand. "This arrangement sounds odd. Should Caroline agree?"

Stockmar held up a finger. "I want the best for you both, and the stage is a risky profession. Leopold will give her income for life, but the marriage must be undisclosed. People could come to the wrong conclusion."

"We shall give it some thought." Mrs. Bauer bit her lip. "Of course, we need the money, and he treated us kindly."

"You must decide if you trust me to manage your affairs." Stockmar stood. "This will ensure your future. You know Caroline will not be beautiful forever."

"Can Mama stay with me when we marry?" Caroline asked hugging herself.

"Oh, yes," Stockmar said.. "He expects your mother to come."

"Caroline," Mrs. Bauer said wagging a finger in her face, "Do not commit until we talk it over. We're both flattered, but we must be wise."

"I'm marrying a prince." Caroline sank onto the bed as visions of diamonds and fancy clothes whisked through her mind.

* * *

The next day

Caroline released a sigh as she gazed about the lush room furnished with overstuffed chairs and a brocade loveseat. A heavy, dark chest sat before a huge, stone fireplace. Mounted deer heads hung on the paneled walls.

"Sir, I present Miss Caroline and her mother, Mrs. Bauer." Stockmar waved the ladies into the room.

Leopold wore an expensive frock coat, white silk cravat, and leather boots. He took several long strides and pulled Caroline into his arms. Right away, he dropped a tender kiss on her lips.

Caroline's body trembled as his lips released hers. She never dreamed this would happen to her.

"Dearest, your ravishing face has haunted me since I saw you last."

He waved her toward the brocade cushions of the loveseat. "Come and sit beside me."

Her gaze glued to his welcoming smile as she joined him.

"Closer, my dear." His eyes seemed to peer into her soul and she shivered.

Only a narrow strip of cushion separated them, and heat blazed throughout her body. She wasn't accustomed to this. After she scooted an inch or so closer, he encircled her with his arm.

"You enchant me. How I shall lavish jewels on you. We shall purchase the finest silks and ermine to transform you into a princess."

Never before had she been at such a loss for words. She looked down at her simple white muslin dress and wished for something nicer. This morning her dress had seemed impressive. Her mother had purchased the embroidered white muslin at an excellent sale.

Then she fashioned it into a gown that matched the latest style—a high waist, and scoop neck. Even the pretty lace sewn along the edge of her sleeves seemed paltry next to his wool and silk.

"Picture this, my love. We sit together in a country home. The sun streams through the window and the birds sing. A pianist plays a concerto on a huge grand piano. You wear a gown of brocade, sitting on cushions of velvet. My son plays at your feet, while I read you a sonnet to express my love for you."

Stockmar held up a finger. "Unless you ascend to the Greek throne."

The prince shot him a frown.

No. I'm going to marry a prince.

* * *

November 1829

England

Caroline gulped as the prince's carriage pulled up to her cottage. All afternoon she practiced her speech from the velvet loveseat. Now that Leopold arrived, her stomach dropped to her heels.

She peeked out the curtains. Enveloped by coats and numerous scarves, he looked like a walking mummy. "Mama, he looks ridiculous. He's so afraid he'll get sick."

Her mother made her usual clucking sound. "Don't be too harsh. The older we are, the easier we succumb to illness, dear."

"Nevertheless, I shall speak my mind." Caroline inhaled. "The man pays no attention to me, and it's unbearable. He made such pretty promises before the wedding ceremony. Did he mean any of them?"

Footsteps sounded in the foyer.

"Caroline!" His voice boomed, making her grind her teeth. "I must go right to the fire. I detest this biting wind. Come for my things."

"Good evening! I hope you are well." Caroline exaggerated her kindness as she offered a curtsy.

He stared.

"Leopold." Caroline kept her voice light. "I missed you."

"Enough!" he bellowed and yanked out his eyeglass.

His cold gaze made Caroline shudder.

"You have prettier hair than Charlotte, but she had a nicer complexion. Your nose is smaller, and your figure is better. But her eyes were much more charming." He flicked his hand as if pushing her away. "However, Princess Louise surpasses you both."

"What? Who is she?" Caroline blinked and her knees wobbled.

"Her father is the King of France," he said. "I shall marry her when I obtain the throne of Greece."

"What?" Caroline's mouth fell open. "How dare you search for a wife? You are married to me!"

"A king needs a royal consort," he said, raising his eyebrows. "You are a commoner."

"Greece? Did you say Greece?" She stopped. "I thought you didn't get the throne."

"I am still negotiating," he said, putting his hand on his chest. "I feel sure they are preparing to make me an offer"

"I demand a divorce."

"No!" Leopold shook his head and turned his back to her.

"Why not?" She rushed toward him and seized his arm.

"I am not finished with you." He pulled free from her grasp and brushed off his coat.

"You are so cruel." Tears blurred her vision. Her trembling hands clenched the red silk of her skirt. "I am not a princess, but I am a person—with feelings."

He raised an eyebrow. "I noticed."

She stomped to her bedroom.

* * *

Caroline sat at the kitchen table across from her mother and

Stockmar. She glared at her untouched breakfast. His gaze seared her face, but she refused to apologize for puffy blood-shot eyes and reddened face.

"You gave an exceptional performance last night, Cousin." Stockmar sighed. "But really, Caroline, I thought you knew better than to tackle the prince yourself."

"We understood that Leopold lost the throne," Mrs. Bauer said.

"Yes." Stockmar looked down and took a deep breath. "Leopold failed, but he continues to negotiate."

"You … knew this?" Caroline looked up.

"I did." He raised his chin. "I hoped that his love for you would keep him happy. If you bore children, his love would be assured."

Caroline burst into tears. How could he find her a failure?

"Neither of us slept last night." Mrs. Bauer patted Caroline's back.

"I'm sorry," Stockmar reached for her hand. "I'll do what I can."

"I want a divorce." Caroline hiccuped and blotted her tears with a limp handkerchief.

"Leopold has no plans to divorce." Stockmar's face hardened.

"But he said —"

"He does not have a throne, and he wants a wife." Stockmar said.

Caroline threw up her hands.

"What should we do?" Mrs. Bauer asked, reaching for a fresh-handkerchief.

He turned toward the door and pointed toward himself. "You must trust me."

"We have done that." Caroline sniffed. "Leopold never kept his promises. He uses me."

"You should continue to trust me. I shall be in touch," he said, raising his voice. He darted from the room.

Caroline dropped her head on the table as all hope crashed about her.

"Hmm." Fritz looked sad as he read.

Vicky watched him for a moment. She didn't want him embroiled in more controversy. That tended to exhaust him and his throat worsened. If they returned now, Fritz would lose all his upward progress while arguing with family and politicians. She and Fritz waited for years to rule, and she wanted him well to do it. All through his illness she labored hard to keep Fritz fighting. German doctors often persuaded him he had little time left. If he listened to those doctors, he'd already be dead.

"I am the heir, and they want me to be there—just in case." Fritz lay back on his pillow.

Vicky rose and paced along the Oriental carpet as she gazed at the gilded carvings on the domed ceiling. "We have finally found someone who can cure you, but they insist on taking you from him. Do they want you to die? Or is it because you are going to an English doctor, not a German?"

"Our politicians don't hate Englishmen, Vicky." Fritz shook his head. "With my father's health so fragile, they want me in the country. From their point of view, it makes sense. I would take up the reins of government. This letter is the strongest appeal yet. In fact, they almost threaten us."

"That is why I brought the letter at once." She made a fist.

Fritz sat up and swung his legs over the edge of the bed. "Perhaps we should start making plans to leave."

"No." Vicky rushed toward him. "You are too close to recovery now, you must not return just as the cool weather comes in."

"What then?" Fritz spread his hands. "I cannot stay away forever."

She leaned over and caressed his thin cheek. "We'll return once you are completely well. You have had too many relapses. This time we must be more cautious."

He tapped the paper he'd dropped on the bedside table. "And

what shall we do about these demands?"

"Tell them we are on our way." Vicky walked to a Walnut secretary and retrieved a document. "I found a lovely cottage in Italy where we can rest several more months. Warm weather there will aid your recovery, and we will not be in England."

"Vicky, dear, I do not dislike England." Fritz eased himself back onto the bed.

"They do!" Her hands clenched as she recalled clashes with newspapers, doctors, and politicians. If she could only get them to understand how much she had to offer. Why would they resent someone who wanted to bring the country into the nineteenth century? But despite all her persuasion, they clung to their old-fashioned ways. "They distrust me because I am not German, and they despise English doctors."

"No one dislikes you, dear wife. My subjects may be jealous of the doctors here, but they think well of you."

She sat down on the bed and caressed his cheek. Her beloved must recover. How would she live without him? "Do you feel ready to return?"

"No."

She waited for him to continue. He must make this decision by himself. Everyone accused her of making him do what she wanted, but she only expressed her opinion.

Muscles around his jaw tightened. "Make plans to go to Italy. Both of us can rest a bit more before we go home."

Vicky laughed and leaned over to give him a passionate kiss. *Now I shall get him well.*

* * *

November 1887

Sam Remo, Italy

Vicky tossed another glance at Fritz while squeezing her lace

candle in her hand clattered onto the wooden floor.

"Wilhelm!" Vicky's mouth fell open as the fall snuffed the candle's flame. "Look what you did."

"Willy, do not treat your mother like that," Fritz commanded. His eyebrows lowered, his eyes blazed, veins protruded in his face and neck.

"This is a waste of my time." Wilhelm turned toward the door. "Grandfather will sign the document giving me the authority—"

"In his condition father would sign anything," Fritz shook his fist in the air. Suddenly, he swayed and began to cough. Fritz collapsed onto the damask cushions of the sofa.

Vicky's legs wobbled, but she dashed toward him and patted his back.

"Well, this proves the press is right." Wilhelm curled his lip. "Papa is not able to rule."

"Wilhelm, stop now." Vicky shouted.

"He is dying!" Wilhelm moved close to her face. "Did you hear that? He is dying of cancer."

Vicky waved him aside and turned to Fritz. Her heart hammered in her chest as she put her arm around her husband.

Fritz sat slumped over, coughing and wheezing. His palm covered his mouth, and blood oozed between his fingers.

Nausea rose and Vicky ground her teeth. She refused to succumb. If only her son hadn't picked this moment to fight. She yanked the bell pull several times.

Wilhelm flung open the door and marched out of the room.

Greta, a lady-in-waiting, walked in yawning. "Do you need help?"

Vicky nodded. "Yes. It's an emergency. Please wake Doctor Bergmann." Despite his German heritage, this physician worked with them. He agreed to stay with Fritz in Italy while he recovered.

Dressed in a housecoat with his hair askew, the doctor arrived, rubbing his eyes. "I must do an exam. We must get him to bed."

Two staff members supported Fritz as he walked to his bed.

Vicky paced and tried to remember quotes from her favorite philosophers to share with her husband. They must overcome this disease so he could rule.

Dr. Bergman frowned. "Your Highness, I stopped the bleeding so the immediate problem is under control. But I see a new growth, and it looks serious. We must wire Dr. Mackenzie right away."

If only I never married Fritz. After coming to Germany, my tranquil life came undone.

She cringed at her own thoughts and collapsed in a chair, sobbing.

* * *

March 1888

Berlin

Vicky closed the bedroom door. Her hand trembled as she pulled out her handkerchief. Muscles in her neck and back ached. How long must she fight the same battle?

The housekeeper entered. "It's Doctor Mackenzie, Ma'am. I knew you'd want to see him right away."

She stood. "Yes. Send him in."

Dr. Mackenzie walked in, his brow creased. "Good afternoon, Empress."

The new title still sounded unfamiliar. Her father-in-law passed away, allowing her husband to ascend to the Prussian throne. If only he could rule, but he had little stamina. "Doctor, I hope you have good news."

"Let's sit down. This is going to take awhile."

A shiver ran up Vicky's back. A doctor with a serious face who wanted to talk meant bad news. But she didn't expect great news. Fritz looked terrible. If only she could fall asleep and not worry about the future. "Doctor, I'm quite tired, and you are more like family. Please sit."

"I can give you something to help you rest."

"No." She licked her lips. Sleeping without being disturbed would be like giving candy to her horse. But she knew her duties. Who else would care for Fritz? "I have to stay alert, even at night."

"That's fine." Mackenzie nodded. "But let me know if you change your mind."

Get to the point. She abhorred people who traveled around an issue trying to avoid speaking the words. Keep it concise was her motto. "What news do you bring?"

"As you know, the lesion I found appeared different from what I saw in the past."

"Yes." She took a deep breath. "And you did a biopsy."

"Indeed, Ma'am." He shifted in his chair, as if uncomfortable. "I'm sorry to bring bad news, but I will be honest. The original tumor appeared to be from excessive speaking. This new one appeared to be carcinoma."

"Go on." She was getting warm while waiting for him to give her something new.

"I sent the sample out for testing to several laboratories in both England and Germany." He rubbed the back of his neck. "None of them came back as malignant."

"Yet my husband grows worse." Her hands squeezed the handkerchief as if it were her mortal enemy. "Then what's my husband's diagnosis?"

"I refuse to name it cancer if the tests come back negative." He rubbed his hands together. "I'm a man of science, not intuition."

She ran a hand over her eyes, hoping they'd stop burning. "The press has called it cancer since long before we met you."

"I know that." He looked down.

"What about treatment? He's getting weaker."

"If the growth continues to enlarge, we'll have to insert a cannula so he can breathe."

She slapped her hand over her mouth as sobs poured from her body. Her willpower kept her going for months. It finally broke. How degrading to weep. She wrenched with every exhale.

A hand touched her shoulder.

The doctor didn't leave. Perhaps he would stay until she gained control. Minutes passed and her convulsive weeping subsided. Sniffles replaced her sobs. "I am sorry, doctor. I do have questions."

"You've been tense for a long time. I read German newspapers. They say the Emperor is dying because he refused the right care from German doctors." He resumed his chair. "How can I help you?"

"I prefer to talk about Fritz." Her voice cracked, and she swallowed several times to moisten her throat. "German doctors want to remove his voice box. Fritz refused. He can't rule without speaking."

"How much can he do now?"

Vicky placed a hand at her neck. "He works an hour or so on his good days. I lay out his work to save his time and energy. Of course I make sure he deals with the crucial issues first."

"I shall do what I can to help." He rose, as if planning to leave.

Vicky stood too. "Would you like to see him?"

"Yes." He moved toward the door. "I shall examine him and suggest further treatments."

"His bedroom is in the other wing." She wrung her hands. "I come here when I need to cry."

"Are you sure I can't prescribe something for you?"

The doctor needed a patient, and Fritz needed him. She pulled the bell. "I shall have someone escort you to the Emperor."

If only she could remedy the situation. After all her father's training, she could run the country. Could she conceal her husband's

Dona stood and edged toward the door, as if she planned to slip out. "This sounds like blasphemy."

Wilhelm burst in. "Dona, let's go. Seckendorff insisted we leave, but I will return. This house will be mine soon, and I will find the evidence that they are hiding."

"Good bye, Wilhelm," Vicky whispered.

These pitiful people who needed to rely on God. He could not be good and kind. Otherwise, God wouldn't have let Father die when she was so young. She was just twenty-one. He was her mentor, and she loved him. No one could be so cruel.

Papa depended on God and prayed all the time. Perhaps his weakness caused his early death. Unthinkable! Her lips twitched as tears slid down her face.

"Your Majesty, can we do anything to help?" Greta stepped forward and Hilda entered behind her.

"See that the maids straighten the library." Vicky crossed her arms and hugged herself. "Losing my husband is enough to bear. But then my own son comes and damages my home. I cannot bear to see the destruction he left behind."

"Hilda, I would like you to contact an English clergyman named William Boyd Carpenter. Look in my papers and find his address. Send a wire and invite him to come here."

Vicky sighed and rubbed her hands over her eyes. She hoped Reverend Carpenter could visit. Talking to a modern clergyman, one who understood science would lift her burden.

But now she'd escape to her sanctuary.

She turned and strolled to the section of the house used only by the family and stopped at a heavy old oak door. With a furtive look up and down the hall, she extracted a key from her skirt pocket. The hinges creaked and groaned as she pushed open the door.

Vicky kept the nursery as pristine as if her children still used

didn't foster calmness. The EMTs fired questions. "Does he have high blood pressure? Does he have diabetes? Has he ever had seizures?"

She understood their line of thinking. They wanted to make sense of this seizure. Each man asked the same questions again and again. Didn't they listen? Besides, she wished they'd grab him off the floor and get him in the ambulance. Instead, they stood by while he woke, a little at a time.

"What is going on?" Ray sat up and glanced around. His face creased, lips turned downward.

She made eye contact with him. "You had a seizure, Ray."

"What are those flashing lights?" Ray spat, his face growing red. "Who are these men?"

She touched his arm. "I called the ambulance. You had a seizure."

Ray tucked his chin and pointed at the pastor. "Why is he here?"

John spoke up, "You're sick, Ray."

His lack of cooperation and anger bothered her. That wasn't typical.

An EMT pulled her to the side. "It's okay, ma'am. It's called post tic. After a seizure people can't recall recent events and stay confused awhile. Without that symptom, doctors won't diagnose a seizure. Start walking and see if he'll go with you."

"We need to get you to the hospital," one EMT said.

"Why? I don't know what's going on." His voice had an edge.

She headed for the front door. "Come with me, Ray."

"Why? Someone tell me why I should."

"Come on, honey." She motioned with her hands. If only he would trust her. "Follow me."

Inch-by-inch she coaxed him to the porch. Once there, several men lifted him onto a stretcher and loaded him into the ambulance.

The EMTs demanded she choose the closest hospital, but their doctor didn't practice there. She understood their concern for speed, but she directed the driver to the hospital her doctor used.

As the ambulance drove off, lights flashing, her mind kept reviewing the facts and pushing aside the tension in her chest and throat. She kept listing causes of seizures. A brain tumor? Surely not.

When they arrived, Ray lay back in the bed, putting his hands behind his head. "I feel so much better."

If only that would last. He'd been sick for six days, but he felt great once his temperature dropped. Cynthia filled out paperwork and answered a multitude of questions.

"Hello, Mr. Simmons." A lady doctor stepped up to his bed in the ER. "How are you feeling?"

"The balance sheet doesn't work, and I have to fix it." He turned his face away.

Alarm bells went off in Cynthia's mind. In a neurological event, a patient's level of consciousness is the most important indicator. His mind sank fast. They faced a serious illness.

She stepped forward. "I'm his wife. Ray's a CPA, and I guess he's confused."

"That's okay." She offered her hand to me. "I'm Dr. Walker. My specialty is infectious disease."

Cynthia related all the pertinent information. Dr. Walker posed a million more questions about where he'd been and what he'd been doing and traveling. Cynthia knew the reasons for the queries, but her heart ached. Early tests came back normal, and then she told the ER doctor Ray had problems recalling words. That's when he ordered a spinal tap.

Blood work, spinal tap, CT scan, EEG—familiar tests that should be done to strangers.

Finally Dr. Walker walked in and smiled. "Mrs. Simmons, we found white blood cells in the spinal fluid. Your husband has encephalitis. Right now he's alert and responding when we talk to him, and that's quite good. He'll be in the hospital for at least three days."

"I understand. Earlier this week our family doctor diagnosed him with the flu, and I—"

Her smile vanished. "He never had the flu. It was encephalitis."

"Oh. That isn't good." Six days of such an infection was quite dangerous. Her husband's intelligence gave so much to their family and the church. Would he recover enough to use his mind again?

* * *

The doctor put him into an intermediate intensive care unit, and they wanted Cynthia to stay since they worried about seizures. Hospital staff came in all night running tests. She didn't sleep at all.

The next morning a neurologist entered. He marched up to Ray. "What's your name? How old are you? Where are you?"

Ray frowned. "My … name … "

Doctors always asked questions to assess his neurological status. She tried giving Ray clues, but they never worked. This doctor showed no consideration. His tone and bearing annoyed her. Ray could respond, but not as fast as this man expected.

His expression was hard and cold. "Mrs. Simmons, may I speak with you outside?"

Her skin tingled. The man's expression bothered her. "Sure."

Just outside of Ray's room, he turned to face her. "You need to understand your husband is very sick. I see both expressive and receptive language issues, and his lab work is horrendous. He won't go home for at least six months."

How would they survive without his salary?

"We'll need to send him to a facility to teach him to walk, dress, tie his shoes, and talk. This is a long-term situation. Prepare yourself."

He could do all that yesterday, and I don't think it's gone. She swallowed back anger and fear as the doctor stalked away. Ray fought a serious illness, but numbers in a chart do not tell the entire

Thank you."

* * *

One sunny morning, Cynthia walked into Ray's hospital room, her arms filled with books to read. A friend from church stood by Ray's bed, helping him with shaving. "Good morning."

"Good morning." He gave her a piercing look. "What's wrong with me?"

"Your brain is infected. It's called encephalitis."

"My brain?" A deep frown creased his brow. "How can that be? That's not good. In fact it's scary."

"Yes." Cynthia put her things away and straightened his sheets. Would he keep asking this time? Or did he understand?

"How on earth did I get this? How long have I been here?"

"We don't know how you got it. You've been here six days."

"Six days?" He closed his eyes and shook his head. "The bill will be terrible. I'll be so far behind. Have you called my boss?"

"Yes. Your boss visited you earlier this week."

"Really?"

A nurse came in to take his blood pressure. She frowned. "It's a bit high today."

He understands his diagnosis. That's progress.

The occupational therapist cleared him for daily living skills, and they began walking to regain his strength. Finally, after eleven days in the hospital, he came home with a pic line for IV medications. He was better, but he had a long way to go.

* * *

A few days before Ray's illness, Cynthia's dad, Mr. Thomas, called from Chattanooga. He reported her mother sleeping a lot. Several years prior, doctors diagnosed her with a rare form of dementia called Lewy Body Disease. Cynthia's stomach tightened since excessive sleeping could be a dangerous sign. She said nothing,

since her dad became upset easily. He acted as Mom's primary care giver, and he needed to stay calm.

Somehow Cynthia's Dad heard Ray was seriously ill. He panicked. Her mother experienced a minor fall and an ER doctor prescribed medicine for pain. Mr. Thomas lost his cool every time her discomfort increased. Cynthia's kids handled lots of frantic calls from her father while Ray stayed in the hospital. They listened to his fears and recommended the medicine the doctor prescribed.

Later Cynthia discovered Mrs. Thomas fell several times during Ray's hospital stay. Terrified of the changes in his wife, he called church friends with each accident. Once his friends called a firemen to scoop her back in bed.

After Ray arrived home, the phone rang, and Cynthia recognized the call from Chattanooga. "Hello?"

"Is this Mrs. Simmons?" A female voice spoke and it wasn't her mother.

"Yes. Who are you?"

"I'm a nurse from Home Health Care. Your mother broke her hip. What hospital would you recommend?"

Cynthia paused as her heart rate went wild. She glanced at her husband. He still had the pic line, and IV medications around the clock. His appointments to speech therapy and various doctors kept her busy. Plus, he suffered from numerous partial seizures. She was trying to get the doctor to prescribe more seizure medication. Under normal circumstances, she'd manage mother's care, but she couldn't dig herself out of the avalanche. Where was her father? Why can't he make decisions? "Hospital?"

"Is Memorial Hospital okay?" The nurse asked.

"Yes." Thank goodness. No names popped into her mind, regardless of how hard she tried.

She hung up and brainstormed until she found friends to sit with her parents in the hospital.

* * *

Ray worked a little at home every day and often needed to go into his downtown office. But the law doesn't allow a grand mal seizure patient to drive for six months. So Cynthia drove Ray to the office several times a week. He stayed an hour or so at a time. His mind turned off, and he'd have to stop working.

One Saturday she sat in the conference room in Ray's office, while he worked in the other room. Her cell phone rang. "Hello?"

"Hey Cyndi. It's Dad. They weighed your mother this morning. She's lost a lot of weight."

Her insides turned to jelly. She knew mother was declining fast.

"They want to put in a feeding tube." Dad paused. "What do you think?"

"That's appropriate. She's been sick almost constantly since her hip surgery, and she's lost ground."

Cynthia managed to stay calm on the phone, but she burst into tears afterward. Her head understood the end loomed closer, but the news stung.

She hurried down to Ray's office. "Dad just called. The nursing home wants to put in a feeding tube. That's not good. She's probably dying."

He stared at her. That morning he'd been restless and irritable—unlike the man she married.

Cynthia sat there and cried alone, as Ray's gaze bored through her.

Under normal circumstances, Ray would embrace her, but he wasn't well either. After such an illness the brain required months to heal. That explained his response, but Cynthia ached inside, feeling alone.

* * *

It took Ray four years to establish a routine, get his seizures under control, and learn to manage his emotions. During that time, several other serious family issues engulfed them. Cynthia's mind stayed on alert. Her mother died, and months later, her father became ill. She moved him into town and emptied her childhood home shortly before he died.

At times she longed for life to return to normal and wondered why God didn't stop the landslide. Where was he?

One day it occurred to her. Friends from church came alongside, brought food and had a special prayer meeting when Ray was hospitalized. Often an acquaintance at church would stop Cynthia and say she was praying. God was there and revealed himself through his church.

Epilogue

A number of months after Ray left the hospital, Cynthia took him to a follow-up visit with their family doctor. He told them most people who contracted encephalitis six days prior to diagnosis either died or spent the rest of their life crippled. Instead Ray had only two lingering side effects: memory loss for words and heightened emotions. Ray ranked in the upper three percent of recovering patients and returned to work with minimal adjustments. Praise the Lord!

2 Corinthians 2:14 "But thanks be to God, who always leads us in His triumph in Christ and manifests through us the sweet aroma of the knowledge of Him in every place." (NAS)

Questions for Thought and Discussion

Chapter One: Royal Crisis

1. Katherine married the king even though she didn't want to. Let's study God's plan for marriage and compare to what you learned about the king and his wife. Read Genesis 1:28 and list the verbs. (These verbs are commands.) Who was supposed to fulfill each command?

2. Read Genesis 2:19-20. How long do you think it took for Adam to name the animals? Why might God have chosen to have Adam do that? What did God say about Adam?

3. Now read verses 21-24. What does this teach you about marriage?

4. Read Ephesians 5:15-24. God gives a reason for his commands. What is it? What is God's command to the wife?

5. Read Ephesians 5:25-27 and list the verbs. What is the husband commanded to do?

6. List the verbs in Ephesians 5:28-29. What is the husband

commanded to do?

7. Did the king obey these commands?

8. Read Romans 2:11. What does this tell you?

9. Based on what you read, compare the king's actions to God's design for the husband. If you could talk to the king, what would you say to him?

Chapter 2: Mortal Danger

1. The Duchess and her husband feared the queen might sentence them to death. Since both of them were believers, they'd go to heaven. Why not submit to death? Read Leviticus 19:15 for an answer.

2. Look up the definition of injustice in the dictionary. Describe what it is in relation to Catherine and Bertie's situation.

3. Exodus 21:23-24 teaches proportional justice. That is, the punishment fits the crime. The founding fathers of our nation based our judicial system on this idea. We instinctively know if someone doesn't treat us appropriately. That's how God designed us. Based on this, what do you think about the king banning certain books?

4. Read Ezra 7:10. What does this teach about reading and studying?

5. Let's read about the role of government in Romans 13. Start with verses one and two. Where does authority come from?

6. What do verses three and four tell you about the reason for government?

7. Particularly note this phrase in verse 3. "...For rules are not a cause for fear for good behavior..." This verse clearly states that rulers do not have the right to punish good behavior. Instead it is "...an avenger who brings wrath on the one who does evil..." What good behavior did Queen Mary seek to punish?

8. Read Proverbs 29:7. What should Queen Mary be concerned about?

9. Read Exodus 30:34-38. These are ceremonial laws given to the Jewish people regarding the use of incense. Why would God punish so severely for misuse of this item? Bring the ideas of justice into your answer.

Chapter 3: Contagion

1. Why was Katie hesitant to care for the sick vagrant? Did she have a valid point?

2. Dr. Luther never left Wittenberg during a plague. Instead he instructed his wife to turn their home into a hospital to care for the sick. In fact, Christians opened many hospitals in America's early days. From James 2:15-16 and Deuteronomy 10:18 give some ideas why that happened.

3. Philippians 2:2-3 gives us negative commands. What do these verses tell us not to do?

4. You'll find a positive command in Philippians 2:3-7. (Have this mind means, "think like this.") How does he instruct us to think? What is Christ's example?

5. Read Matthew 22:39. Does other-centered thinking mean we don't care for ourselves? Why or why not?

6. How do you decide when to risk your life for someone else? Isaiah 41:17. Psalm 23.

Chapter 4: Starting Again

1. Katie returned to Wittenberg after the war to reopen her boarding house. Was that the right thing to do? Read I Timothy 5:8.

2. Because of ancient laws, the people of Wittenberg didn't want Katie to be independent despite the fact that she could. Read these verses and describe what the Bible says about the widow. Isaiah 1:17, Zech 7:10, Job 31:16.

3. Read Galatians 6:5. (Note the word "load" means appropriate

responsibilities.) What light does this shed on Katie's situation?

4. Reread the creation mandate in Genesis 1:28. Does this leave the woman out? How can you be sure?

5. What direction does I Timothy 5:3-6 give about widows?

6. If Katie's brother had not helped, what would you advise Katie to do? Jeremiah 2:13.

Chapter 5: The Price of Freedom

1. Louise was hurt by her husband's actions. All of us have an inborn sense of justice. Our founding fathers spoke of them in our nation's earliest documents. Read Proverbs 31:9 and discuss the origin of those thoughts.

2. Read Exodus 20:12-17 and list what rights God defends in this passage.

3. Especially note verse 15 in the passage above. Contrast what this verse teaches with Communism. Read Habakkuk 1:2-4 and note the wording in verse 4. Describe how the prophet feels and why.

4. Read Genesis chapter 16 on Hagar. Especially note verse 13. What did Hagar call God? What does that mean?

5. Did Sarai value her maid? Did God value Hagar? How do you know?

6. How might that story help Duchess Louise?

7. Do you agree or disagree with the way Louise chose to get freedom? Why?

Chapter 6: A Better Man

1. Charles offended Susannah when he forgot and left her in the crowd. Compare his actions with the people in Genesis 6:5.

2. Read Numbers 15:27-28. How does this apply to Spurgeon? Contrast the above passage with Numbers 15:30.

3. Read Genesis 9:6 and Romans 14:15. Explain why we should

respect others.

4. Read Matthew 18:15 and discuss how Susannah might handle her husband's mistakes after they marry.

5. Read Genesis 3:8-13. Compare Spurgeon's actions with Adam and Eve's. Read Genesis 2:20. God made woman to be a suitable helper to her husband. Discuss ways that Susie could help Spurgeon with his weak areas after they marry.

Chapter 7: A Handful of Peppermint Candy

1. The war made Ellen fearful and anxious. Read Genesis 2:17 and James 4:1-2. List several reasons people can't get along.

2. Reverend McCallie stayed in Chattanooga during the war to minister to soldiers and citizens who came through. Compare Psalm 91:11-12 and Romans 1:14-16. Based on theses passages, do you agree or disagree with his decision?

3. Read Deuteronomy 8:1-3. From verse three, describe what Ellen needed most.

4. What can we learn from Psalm 41:1-2? Do these verses promise you won't die in a war? Now look at John 10:27-28. How might these verses impact Ellen?

5. Now examine Isaiah 43:2. What promises do you see here? Does God always keep us from trouble? Why or why not?

6. What does Romans 5:3-5 teach us about trials?

Chapter 8: Foreign Country

1. Contrast what Emilie wanted with what Abraham wanted in Hebrews 11:8-10.

2. Compare Deuteronomy 5:17, Joshua 9:24, and Joshua 10:24. . Is it wrong to take a life during war?

3. Discuss God's thoughts on widows from James 1:27 and Psalm 146:9.

Questions

1. Read John 11:35, Psalm 56:8, and Matthew 12:20. Describe how God views a grieving person.

2. How should a believer grieve according to I Thessalonians 4:13-14?

3. Based on 2 Corinthians 6:14-16 explain why someone who trusted Christ should not marry an unbeliever. What problems did Emilie experience?

4. Emilie lived during a time of great upheaval. The war split good friends and family members. Read Ephesians 2:19-22 and discuss what Emilie could hold on to.

Chapter 9: The Journey

1. Once Alice left home, she was dismayed to discover that her fellow Germans did not think as deeply as her father, and she sought out David Frederick Strauss. His ideas made her question her faith. Read 1John 4:1, John 3:1-2, and Acts 17:11. Is it wrong to question what you've been taught? Should you believe everything you hear from a minister?

2. Go further with Hebrews 6:1. What does God want us to do?

3. What is the sign of the resurrection? Read John 2:18-21 and Matthew 12:39-40

4. How important is this sign? Romans 1:4.

5. Look up the word resurrection and write the definition. Read Luke 24:36-43. List proofs of the resurrection from those verses.

6. Paul wrote the book of I Corinthians about 53A.D., which was about twenty years after the death and resurrection of Christ. With that in mind, read I Corinthians 15:3-9. How many people saw Jesus alive after his crucifixion? Discuss the strength of this evidence.

is the outcome of sin? How does that impact our world?

2. Read Matthew 6:34 to discover what we will find every day. How does that make you feel?

3. Since life brings heartache, we could easily despair. What does God tell us to do instead? Read James 1:2-6. What is the outcome of tribulation?

4. For several years, Cynthia found herself beset with serious trials that required good judgment and wisdom she didn't have. What promise do you find in James 1:5? List ways you might apply that verse.

5. Growing up in a Christian family, Cynthia often felt emotions were taboo. Compare Matthew 26:38-39 and Hebrews 12:2. Do these verses contradict? If not, what do they teach?

6. Read Romans 8:22-23. In verse 23, find the negative truth and the positive truth. How do they go together? How might this verse help someone during suffering?

7. Often people say God wants people to be happy. Read Romans 8:18 and James 1:3-4. What do these verses teach God wants for us?

8. During this difficult time, Cynthia found Isaiah 42:3-4. These verses describe the Messiah. The passage is repeated in Matthew 12:18-21. What does this tell you about Jesus?

9. Cynthia discovered God comforted her through the church. Read Acts 2:42, I John1:7, and Ephesians 5:18-20. Discuss what fellowship means and how this applies to your life.

10. Study Romans 8:35-39. What positive truth does God teach there? Describe how you feel after meditating on that truth.

CPSIA information can be obtained
at www.ICGtesting.com
Printed in the USA
FSHW010835130619
58958FS